First published in Great Britain in 2014 by Comma Press
www.commapress.co.uk

'Spare Me, Copacabana!' first appeared in *Para Copacabana, Com Amor* (Editora
Oito e Meio, 2013). 'Something Urgently' first appeared in *Romances e Contos
Reunidos* (Companhia das Letras, 1997). 'The Biggest Bridge in the World' first
appeared in *O Homem Vermelho* (Civilização Brasileira, 1977). 'Song of Songs' first
appeared in *Vinte Contos e uns Trocados* (Grupo Editorial Record, 2011). 'Lucky
was Sandra' first appeared in *Domingos sem Deus* (Grupo Editorial Record,
2011). 'Strangers' first appeared in *50 Contos e 3 Novelas* (Companhia das Letras,
2007). 'Decembers' first appeared in *Porto do Rio - do Início ao Fim* (Editora
Rovelle, 2012). 'The Woman who Slept with a Horse' first appeared in *A Mulher
que Transou com o Cavalo e Outras Histórias* (Língua Geral, 2012). 'I Love You' first
appeared in *Escrevendo No Escuro* (Editora Rocco, 2011). 'Places, in the Middle of
Everything' first appeared in *Por Escrito* (Companhia das Letras, 2014).

A CIP catalogue record of this book is available from the British Library.

ISBN 1905583680
ISBN-13 978 1905583683

The publisher gratefully acknowledges the support of Arts Council England.

Supported by
**ARTS COUNCIL
ENGLAND**

Obra publicada com o apoio do Ministério da Cultura do Brasil / Fundação
Biblioteca Nacional.
Work published with the support of the Ministry of Culture of Brazil / National
Library Foundation.

MINISTÉRIO DA CULTURA
Fundação BIBLIOTECA NACIONAL

Set in Bembo 11/13 by David Eckersall
Printed and bound in England by Berforts Information Press Ltd.

THE BOOK OF
RIO

Edited by
Toni Marques
& Katie Slade

Contents

CONTENTS

Introduction

RIO DE JANEIRO was unintentionally founded as the result of territorial occupation strategies devised for the purpose of expanding the Portuguese Empire. Brazil was never originally meant to become a nation.

On 1st January 1502, a Portuguese fleet under the command of Pedro Álvares Cabral, arrived in this unnamed bay and claimed it in the name of the crown, christening the bay (not actually a river) after the month of its discovery. Despite an otherwise successful offensive along this enormous coastline (Brazil's coast stretches over 4600 miles), the settlers were unable to win over this particular region's native tribes. More conflicts were to follow. During the mid-sixteenth century, other European powers advanced into the recently-colonised region, notably the French who formed the France Antarctique colony (in what we now know as Rio) in 1555 as a haven for persecuted Huguenots. The Portuguese, anxious to secure their dominance of the land once and for all, fought back, and destroyed the France Antarctique in 1567. As a result of the struggle, Rio de Janeiro was officially born.

The colonisation of Brazil continued for another two centuries, driven by the African slave trade, sugarcane plantations, whale hunting and Catholic missionaries. Then, at the dawn of the nineteenth century, the royal court of Portugal under threat from Napoleonic forces, moved from Lisbon to Brazil, making Rio de Janeiro a unique case in history: a colonial city transformed into an imperial capital, a home-from-home for the Portuguese Royal Family. The move brought scientists, architects, and artists to Brazil, many of them French, but it also attracted the British after Portugal offered to open all its ports around the world to Great Britain if it helped to defeat Napoleon. Rio de Janeiro was now the heart of the kingdom, complete with an international seaport, and became a magnet for a new immigrant labour force. Gradually, the colonial mindset gave way to a cosmopolitan outlook, a viewpoint which later had an impact on the arts and letters that would portray city life.

By this time, Brazilian writers living outside of Rio were acknowledging the influence of the Baroque literary movement in their work, as well as introducing strong satirical and political elements of their own. The nineteenth century saw the rise of the Romantic writers, some of whom were living in Rio, followed by the Realists, the pre-Modernists, the Modernists, and so on. While this rapid change was happening in literature, Brazil was simultaneously cutting its ties with Portugal and becoming its own empire, despite increasing demands from members of the Portuguese nobility that the royal court be returned to Lisbon, and that Brazil remain a colony. Rising tensions between the two nations resulted in the Brazilian War of Independence in 1822, from which Brazil emerged victorious. In 1825, a peace treaty officially recognising Brazil's independence was signed by both sides. However, dissatisfaction with the Brazilian ruling powers lead to years of revolts, rebellions and social and political upheaval. In 1889, Brazil's own monarchy was overthrown by a military coup, and Brazil finally became a republic.

Machado de Assis (1839-1908), arguably Rio's first literary genius, embodied what it was like to be born, live and write in the city during this period. His mother was a Portuguese washerwoman, his father a Brazilian painter of dual heritage. He attended public school but never went to university, managed to rise through the ranks while writing poems and chronicles for newspapers, and finally became a member of elite society. His literary universe embraced high society, the manners of the salon, political intrigue, the anxieties of an emerging urban middle class developing in tandem with an embryonic capitalist state, the poor and downtrodden, and the ironies of life in general. He was able to look at Rio, and Brazil, as a magical realist (the narrator of his novel *The Posthumous Memoirs of Bras Cubas*, 1881, is already deceased), or alternatively as a satirist, a realist, a naturalist, or an impressionist. Machado De Assis' protean literary techniques suggested that life was too complex a subject to only be dealt with through one artistic approach, and his observations on urban life set the benchmark for other Brazilian writers in the years to follow.

João do Rio (1881-1921) and Lima Barreto (1881-1922) are two of the best examples of the fresh urban eyes required by Rio de Janeiro during its so-called 'Belle Époque', when the aspirations of the educated population to live more like Europeans couldn't mask the overwhelming poverty in the city. Do Rio and Barreto's writing rebuffed elitist society and the embroidered language still prevalent in Brazilian literature. Despite Machado de Assis' achievements, Brazilian writers were still drawing on pre-avant-garde European literary styles.

The Modernist movement that erupted in Brazil in 1922 was first and foremost a São Paulo city movement that sought a truly Brazilian way of seeing and telling. Nevertheless, it quickly became popular among Rio-based writers, mostly poets. The best was yet to come regarding novels, the short story and theatre.

Machado De Assis, Barreto and do Rio's efforts combined with the ground-breaking Modernist movement to create a literary city that was now truly, socially diverse. Note, however, that there is no Bossa Nova equivalent in Brazilian literature: no easy-going, smart, sexy, middle-class take on the city's most affluent areas, no mesmerizing picture-postcard natural wonders (Bossa Nova is known for its celebration of Rio's landscapes), no chauvinist look at a given, privileged lifestyle.

A grittier, literary backdoor to the city was offered by Rubem Fonseca (b. 1925), who started writing in the early 1960s. Before him, we had the Brazilian answer to Virginia Woolf, the great Ukranian-born Clarice Lispector, with her inner scavenging of what it was like to be a woman in Rio; and the playwright Nelson Rodrigues, who brought the wild dreams and the repressed sexuality of the average Rio inhabitant to the stage. Born in Minas Gerais but growing up in Rio, Fonseca was the first Brazilian prose writer to bring what some people might call 'non-literary' themes into the equation. When most Rio writers were more concerned with the city's surrounding countryside, Fonseca brought the sheer brutality of urban life to the front row of literature. Imagine Raymond Chandler charting a city full of *favelas,* resentment and people still invisible to most writers: the oddballs, the disenfranchised, the marginalised, the social underdogs.

Fonseca didn't intend to shock, but rather to dissect. Before his first book, the short-story collection *The Prisoners*, no other writer would have dared to describe the streets of Rio at Carnival time through the eyes of a bodybuilder in drag, spoiling for a fist-fight. Like do Rio and Barreto before him, Fonseca knew that Rio was a city behind a city, a place where anything goes, a landscape so cruel and violent that any Bossa Nova song lyrics written about it would sound like a joke. It's fair to say that Fonseca opened all the remaining doors for Rio writers; this was no place for middle-class self-indulgence. Fonseca didn't patronize the poor, or criticise Brazil's slavery past or its civil (1937-1945) and military (1964-1985) dictatorships: bad people were bad people, irrespective of background and context. After Fonseca, everyone was free to try their hand at literally any subject.

Fonseca's literary career began when the people of Rio were still living through the hazy post-War tropical Riviera dream, when Hollywood celebrities sipped champagne at the

Copacabana Palace Hotel and the best nightclubs were in full swing with new musical acts introduced every night. This is the point in the anthology where Cesar Cardoso's 'Spare Me, Copacabana!' finds its place; a story which delicately entwines the fate of the theatrical narrator and of Copacabana itself as we watch their gradual decline from glamour to dereliction. Similar themes are explored in Marcelo Moutinho's 'Decembers', which pays homage to the golden era of Brazil's Rádio Nacional through a story in which a boy begins to question his fading relationship with his reticent grandfather.

Fonseca didn't write about the military dictatorship, but Domingos Pellegrini did when he conceived 'The Biggest Bridge in the World', a story about one of the several military engineering feats that was intended to lead Rio and Brazil to a glittering future, whatever the costs to the construction workers. Of course, every dream may have its nightmarish counterpart, and here we have 'Something Urgently', João Gilberto Noll's subtle father-and-son story about the atrocities being carried out by government agents during the 1960s and 70s, while Copacabana's underworld was still winking at every passer-by.

When the years of military dictatorship finally came to an end, you could be forgiven for thinking that Rio was now a safe and neatly partitioned city. Sérgio Sant'Anna's 'Strangers', in which two house-hunters simultaneously viewing the same apartment discover that it's within shooting distance of a notorious *favela,* cautions us not to jump to simple conclusions: there's a grey area that every Rio citizen knows all too well. No matter where you live, there's a clash between the middle class, the well-to-do, and the forgotten ones. There's no way out. The recent city-wide protests against the World Cup and the Olympic Games, the wasted public money on useless plans, the political corruption, the awful public services, the neglected poverty and everything else are a powerful reminder that there are no enclaves, no gated communities, no sealed-off areas of privilege. There are no clichés here either: women are not topless on the beaches, and men don't sunbathe in thongs all day long as if they were in Ibiza. In fact, many residents find the most famous urban beaches – Copacabana, Ipanema and Leblon – just plain filthy. Many of us positively dislike wearing flip-flops, drinking caipirinhas and watching football matches; some of us badmouth *favelas* and look at poor people as if they were Martians or villains; some of us disdain the sex industry and even get shocked by the sight of young prostitutes and their potential clients strolling along Copacabana's Avenida Atlântica. Some of us hate Carnival time. Many of us wouldn't think to look for insights into the city in a book of fiction.

Mundane, daily life can be just as hard to escape. Citizens may go to love hotels (and Rio's got plenty of them), like in Elvira Vigna's 'Places, in the Middle of Everything' in which a separated couple meet up for the first time in years in a desperate attempt to rekindle their former passions. Then in João Ximenes Braga's 'The Woman who Slept with a Horse', a young, naïve publisher crosses class boundaries when she becomes entangled in a doomed love affair involving supernatural African rituals. And the grass is not always greener as the call-girl narrator of Patrícia Melo's 'I Love You' discovers when she reluctantly becomes involved in the failing marriage of two residents of Leblon, Rio's wealthiest and trendiest neighbourhood.

Rio has always had a reputation as one of the party capitals of the world, but Nei Lopes' somewhat unsettling 'Song of Songs' exposes the evolution, or rather the tragic involution, of the merciless Carnival industry, while Luiz Ruffato's 'Lucky Was Sandra' challenges the stereotypical image of Copacabana as a haven for free bodies and souls, when the eponymous heroine struggles to overcome her working-class background.

This anthology doesn't cover every facet of Rio life (something, of course, no work of fiction ever could). But it can be read as a literary map for those unfamiliar with the city; a map which leads us through Rio's streets story by story and helps us understand a little better what it's actually like to live, work, and grow up here. It's a book about blending and not blending, and Brazil and especially Rio are all about blending and not blending. The South Zone, Rio's cluster of fancy neighbourhoods, can't exist without the rest of the city; the *favelas* can't exist without the rest of the city; the real Rio, whatever it is, can't exist without the foreign vision of men in thongs and topless women. And unfortunately we still can't be a city without the shame of drug-trafficking gangs killing each other, corrupt and incompetent politicians, crooked and murderous cops, an inadequate sewage system, an overcrowded public transport system, throngs of jaywalkers, a multitude of bad drivers, blasé litter-bugs, a vast amount of run-down public schools, a rotten number of unhygienic public hospitals, and so on, and so on.

Rio's nom-de-guerre, however, is still 'Marvellous City'. See for yourself how marvellous it is.

Toni Marques
Rio de Janeiro, April, 2014

RIO DE JANEIRO

Mangueira

Cinelândia

Catete

Dona Marta

Rua Sao Clemente

Botafogo

Copacabana

Ipanema

Leblon

Niteroi

Spare me, Copacabana!

Cesar Cardoso

Translated by Ana Fletcher

OH GOD, THE buzzer again. Spare me, Copacabana! Night crashes in and here we are in front of the mirror. We being me, my make-up, my blushers, my wrinkles, my implants. It can't be him. Not yet. Look at the state of me. I need to concentrate... concentrate. What will he bring me this time? Oh bother! Why won't they leave me alone? I just can't seem to shake people off – it's always been this way. Pass me that cotton wool, go on. You're no use either. Why don't you just swallow down those teeth and get that fake smile out of my sight. You're faker than my ID card. You wouldn't believe the scratches on it. Not even my soul, poor thing, has as many. The first time round I was trying to make myself older, can you imagine? I wanted to get into Vogue, *chèrie*, the chicest nightclub in Copacabana back then. The bouncer looked me up and down. Do you know what he said to me? Nuh-thing. He just pushed me away with the back of his hand. That made my blood boil. I pulled out the knife and slashed those strong features of his. Nothing too serious; just enough so he'd remember.

It does us good to remember. Why won't that buzzer stop? Oh anguish! Look here, don't ruin my nails, you brute! I'd give anything to have him with me now, kissing my feet one more time. You what? I'll have you know these tootsies right here have belonged to Sonia Braga *and* Vera Fisher in TV ads. You don't know anything. Then again, who does know anything around here? Roll up to see the end of the world – best seats in the house. Copacabana is made of sand. It sticks to the body, but slips between the fingers. Once I was leaving that cinema over there at Posto 6, the Caruso; now *that* was a cinema – the armchairs in there! You can't imagine the things you could get up to in one of those armchairs. But the guy I was with only had eyes for the film, which, by the way, was a misery-fest; some woman who hasn't got a pot to piss in finds a partner to enter some dance marathon in… California, I think. There was me thinking I was going to see a musical, something happy, upbeat. I love musicals; humanity learnt how to fly with Santos Dumont, I learnt with Fred Astaire. But where was I? Oh yes, so the contestants who don't die of hunger end up dancing themselves to death. The guy in the main couple snuffs it in the middle of the floor and the woman keeps dancing, carrying the poor sod so she doesn't get disqualified. Endless misery. And what's worse, not funny. But anyway, I'm leaving the Caruso, already fucked off with life at this point, and wouldn't you know it – a crazy woman comes and grabs onto my clothes. Saying she had to kill herself, she had to kill herself, she had to. What's it to me, child? You want to kill yourself? Throw yourself under the first bus that comes by, we've no shortage of buses round here, but let go of my clothes. Do you know how much this blouse cost, darling? I'd die for a shirt like that. I had to show her how things work. Me and my knife. I guarantee you, she ran for a doctor and never thought about doing something so stupid again. But as soon as we got rid of the little crackpot, what does the guy want? To be shown Beco da Fome. Oh my Lord, what was he? Some sort of folklorist? A researcher? I don't need anyone else to get to Beco da Fome – my own legs will carry me. Divine as they are. Back then I used to cross the neighbourhood by foot, on stiletto heels, without tripping over a single one of those Portuguese cobblestones. Sodding things. Come here, put your hand here, forget that damned buzzer, feel my legs. These were on the cover of

Vogue, my dear. But where was I? Oh yes, in Beco da Fome; a couple off their faces at the other end of the bar, and two cops walk in with a whore. I saw straight away things were going south. I felt for the knife under my clothes. The guy in the fucked-up couple smiled, happy to be there, looking around at us for the *saudade* that song talks about. Then yes, the cop faced the poor bastard and said: what are you looking at my woman for? The guy wasn't looking at anything and that whore wasn't even a woman, but that wasn't the point, was it? It's never the point. The cop whipped out a gun and waved that big, silver thing, hot and cold, next to my ear, while he shouted at the fucked-up guy: do you know who you're talking to? I am Brazil! Brazil! And would you believe, that's just what it said on the pocket of his uniform? Sergeant Brazil, stitched on right there. When we see that in the *novelas*,[1] we think they're overdoing it, right? All I know is that Brazil sent the fucked-up couple running. I was left scratching the blade against my thigh, my hands colder than the beers that Thrice With Starch[2] would bring us non-stop, without us even asking for them. Do you remember Thrice With Starch, that nice barman? It's like he was on autopilot. Have another beer – I couldn't even go to the toilet. And didn't it just happen that after Brazil disappeared the shameless bastard couldn't even fuck me, from how scared he was? Oh, Beco da Fome! I never set foot in that cave again. I always get my revenge, you understand?

Hell's teeth! The buzzer again. It can only be him. Oh, my Orishas, and you haven't even finished my hair, you pest! What if he's brought me a wig? What? Nail polish! Don't jinx me. If he turns up here with nail polish I'll make you drink it, you brute! I want a wig. That ride in the sea at dawn is what left my hair this way. That crazy fisherman. He only

1. Or 'telenovelas' – serial TV dramas popular in Latin America, distinct from soap operas for their short-run, usually lasting less than a year.
2. For cariocas or Rio natives, *Três com Goma* is slang for a *malandro* – an old-school hustler. Legend has it Rio gangsters used to get their over-sized suits washed three times with extra starch thrown in.

wanted to fuck on the sand, on the rocks, oh, my Lord! The scraping my arse took because of that wretch. Oh gorgeous man! He knew everything! And he also hated the Portuguese cobbles. He was one of mine. Very much mine. I'm not bothered about him anymore. I had OCD, you know? OCD, you fool. Obssessive Compulsive Disorder. A terribly chic disease. Me and Roberto Carlos have it. I don't know why he doesn't abandon that bloody Urca once and for all and come to live here. Isn't this his place? I could only walk on those Portuguese cobbled pavements in five-two. No, you idiot, it's like a time signature. Five steps on the white stones and two on the black. As a result, I couldn't walk and talk at the same time because I had to pay my own steps so much attention. And that's not to mention the times I had to leap, or stretch out like a flamingo, and everyone around me staring and getting out the way. They think madness is catching. I don't bother with that anymore. I miss him so much. He drowned. A far-fetched story, you know? They even said it was me who pushed the poor sod from Pedra do Leme. Ha! I actually tried to hold on to him. But who could have handled his strength? Only the sea. It swallowed his body, which never turned up. Spinoza called me to testify down at the 12th Precinct. And then to ask me out. But that's another story. He's got a thing for Middle Eastern food and red wine. Urgh! And all he can talk about is work, work, work. Finish that hair already, pest! Oh, Copacabana! Do as he did: take me in a red Cadillac, leaning on the horn all the way along Avenida Atlântica, mocking the doormen at the hotel there. Copacabana, I was your siren once, always smiling, but now – where's the money for a dentist? Old age is spending twice as much and getting half as far. And, on top of that, propping up the family that spent years turning its back on me. My two brothers? One became an evangelical, the other went to the loony bin, poor things. Not a pot to piss in between them and here I am paying the rent. I take my revenge where I can get it, *chèrie*.

But where was I again? Not the wig, not the buzzer, you

sluggard, it was him, the fisherman. I met him at the entrance to Marimbás, the boat club. No, it was at the fishermen's colony. At dawn. That's right. Either the colony or Marimbás. He was coming in with his fish, and I was being sick on the scenery. He came to my rescue. He offered me some fish and I offered myself. Each of us gave what we had and it was love at first sight. The problem is that here in Copacabana you can't believe in the view or in love. We spent a whole year ordering last rounds in Beco da Fome. An obsession he had. I would ask him to take me to Vogue, he would say the place was full of idiots and laugh. On our third anniversary, he turned up at my place with a beautiful dress, it must have cost a whole trawler's worth of fish, a fortune, or at least one of those fortunes that are made and lost over here. He told me to get dressed and didn't say anything else while I prattled away at him, wanting to kill my curiosity. When we stepped out of the lift, he told me we were going to Vogue. Oh, *chèrie*, I felt like crying! But I wasn't fool enough to let my eyes go puffy, was I? We got into that blue Cadillac of his and set off. He drove nice and slow and I savoured every one of those beautiful Portuguese cobblestones. As we got closer, the traffic got worse, all bottled up; I'd never seen anything like it in Copacabana at dawn. I mean, I probably had done, but I've always preferred to forget the things I might know. Forgetting has always been my strong suit, you know? Then we started to hear the firemen's sirens. I couldn't believe it. The day I was finally going to triumph at Vogue... and there was a cursed fire right in my way! Some idiot housewife who forgot that her sodding beans were on the stove. Or a miserable bitch who killed her lover by setting fire to the mattress. The riffraff that block up the streets and gutters of Copacabana. Oh, how vulgar! Until a fireman leaned over the door of the Cadillac and said we had to turn back. I took a deep breath and explained that that was completely impossible. I'm on my way to Vogue, my dear, Vogue! And he told me as if it were the most normal thing in the world that Vogue doesn't exist anymore, that's where the fire is, there's nothing left, not one piano key, it's licked the whole building, it's gone! It was August 13th, a Friday. But I didn't believe it. I opened the door and started running towards the club. There really was nothing left. I mean, there was an American singer bust up on the pavement. He flung himself from the tenth floor. They say he jumped singing 'Ne Me Quitte Pas', which was his big number at the club. I found the doorman, sitting on the curb. The poor creature hugged me, crying, and could only say: what a coincidence! What a coincidence! I think he meant to say what a catastrophe. He rubbed his hand over the scar on his face and cried, that enormous man. They say that up in the North East he used to be a hitman, the best of them. And that that's where he got his scar from. He came to Rio to retire and take it easy, beating and shooting wannabe rich kids at the entrance to the club. Me and the fisherman walked to Beco da Fome, to order a last round, which he hated, but by that time… We drank until the sun came up, red, and walked out, looking at the neighbourhood. I watched Copacabana be born, but I wasn't paying attention when she died. I must have been looking somewhere else.

Oh my Lord, the buzzer again. What if it's him, what if it is? Oh anguish, finish that hair already, come on! Oh, what I wouldn't give for a necklace. One of those that are in fashion right now. No, not that crap they wear on the *novelas*, not that. The one that lives on the neck of that princess of England. So chic. Oh no, the doorbell – what now? Wait! Look through the peephole first. If it's that Candomblé priest from the fifth floor, don't open it. He's obsessed with me. Father Rubem Maria de Oxóssi. What sort of a name is that for a Candomblé priest? The day before yesterday I bumped into him in the lift; he grabbed me to say that Copacabana is going to be destroyed by a tsunami. And what? I just want him to get here before the tidal wave, take me in his arms and do with me what he will. Then, my love, you can chuck me into the first wave that sweeps Prado Júnior. Father Rubem said that the eve of my judgment day had come and that I couldn't see it. And what do you think I am? A turkey, that I should die on the eve of anything? Get off me. I'm going to sing him my closing number is what I'm going to do. It's always the last one I sing, otherwise there's no soul in it. Look at the ring he gave me. No, this one was a gift from the fisherman. Oh, what does it matter who gave it to me you jealous cow? It's not like you'll ever get one. This is amethyst, got it? Amethyst. It was on that wretched day. We fought over Almir, that guy from Pernambuco who played for Flamengo and got into a fight with a whole team from Bangu at Maracanã, remember? They killed him there in Rio Jerez. They said it was because of me. What a joke. That day. We were going to the show at Galeria Alaska, but we argued; I went home and that was it. Then he started drinking *chopps* over at Bar Bico, at Posto 6. He went down to Lucas', on the beach, to drink steinhager; he stopped by Bip Bip, for some beers, but he didn't even stick around to listen to the samba – he went straight on to Caranguejo, to eat crabmeat with hot sauced drizzled all over it, he used to love that. He stopped at Panamá and had champagne with sardines; from there to Adega Pérola, to eat some rollmops with five or six of the twentysomething cachaças[3] they have there. Then he carried on to Pavão Azul, he ate pataniscas[4] with gin, and he went to Baalbek, in Galeria Menescal – the owner always had a bottle of arrak set aside for him. Then, he got to Real Chopp and alternated between some of the hard stuff he liked – Strega, Cinzano and fernet. He dropped in at Cervantes and Shirley. From there he went to Pedra do Leme. They came to call me, but by the time I got there he'd already thrown himself into the sea. The body turned up five days later in Itaipuaçu. I went to identify it. Have you ever seen somebody who's been under water for five days? A body invaded by the sea and the fishes? I spent three months going

3. A distilled spirit made from sugarcane juice.
4. Traditional Portuguese dish consisting of battered, shredded cod.

to the cinema four times a day to forget it. All the ushers knew my name. There aren't any ushers anymore, and soon there won't be any cinemas. And who knows when you and I will be finished too, Copacabana? How many Copacabanas have known me? How many will still come across me, turn away from me, curse me behind my back, pull my hair, scratch me and end up kissing me? This ring here, for example. This is a ruby, you nuisance, a ruby. But there are people who say that's a lie, that it's cheap glass. Nobody knows, do they? Here even a diamond turns into cheap glass. Oh, I'd so like to cross Galeria Alaska on a scooter for the last time. Copacabana, you are life and death singing. Me too, Copacabana – how many times have I died here on your rubbish-strewn corners? How many times have I been happy? And what will come next? The bell. It's him! It's him.

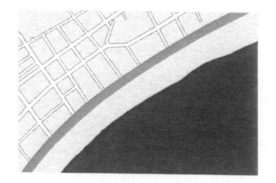

Something Urgently

João Gilberto Noll

Translated by Sophie Lewis

THE EARLY YEARS of life gave me a taste for adventure. My father used to say he didn't know what we were put here for and was always moving on to new work, new women, new locations. My father's most striking characteristic was his endless moving-on. He called himself a bookless philosopher, with only one thing on his side: his mind. At first I thought him merely embittered after being abandoned by my mother when I was still an infant. At that time we were living at the top of Rua Ramiro Barcelos, in Porto Alegre. Every morning my father would take me for a walk in the Praça Julio de Castilhos and teach me the names of the trees. I didn't like just knowing the names; I wanted to know the characteristics of every plant and the region it came from. He would tell me that the world was much more than those plants, that it was also the people walking by and the ones standing about, and that every one of them had their own drama. I would ask to sit on his lap. He would set me on his knees and whistle a mediaeval air that he claimed was his favourite tune. Sitting there on his lap, I would stammer out a few risky thoughts:

'When are you going to die?'

'I won't leave you alone, son!'

He looked at me, visibly troubled, and said that first he would teach me to read and write. He was determined to forget that I knew everything that went on with him. 'Why should I read?' I asked him. 'So you can describe how this tree looks,' he would reply, a bit annoyed by my question. But he soon calmed down.

'When you learn to read, you will, in a way, own everything under the sun, including yourself.'

Towards the end of 1969, my father was sent to prison far away in the state of Paraná. (They said that he had been dealing arms to some group, I don't know which.) At that time he had a place that sold meat and fish in Ponta Grossa and had stopped taking me out for walks.

The day he was arrested, I was dragged out of the shop by a very light-skinned neighbour who said that I would be spending a few days in her house, that my father was going on a journey. I didn't believe a word but acted gullible like a proper child. For what would happen if I were to tell her this was a bunch of lies? How do you handle a child who knows? They put me in a boarding school deep in São Paulo state. The head *padre* looked at me and declared that I would be happy there.

'I don't like it here.'

'You'll get used to it; even find you enjoy it.'

My fellow students taught me to play football, to masturbate and to steal food from the fathers. I got a hard-on and showed it to my classmates. I showed them my haul of stolen apples and sweets. I told them about my father. One of them hated me. My father was murdered, he told me, hatred in his eyes. My father was a gangster, he said, spitting venom from the heart.

I shut up. For talking about my father would require knowledge I didn't have. A letter from him arrived. But the head father did not let me read it; he called me to his study and reported that my father was fine.

'He is fine.'

I thanked the head father the way we always did, whatever the occasion, and left, repeating in the stillest part of myself:

12

'He is fine.'

The boy who hated me sidled up and said that his father had been shot seventeen times.

In our scripture classes, Father Amâncio taught us to say the rosary and to recite ejaculations.

'Salve Maria!' he would exclaim at the beginning of every class.

'Salve Maria!' we boys would reply in unison.

When I was bigger, my father came to fetch me and he had lost one arm. The head father asked me:

'Do you want to go?'

I looked at my father and said that I already knew how to read and write.

'Then one day you will know everything,' he said.

The boy who hated me was standing by the school door when we left. His uniform was freshly washed and ironed.

On the road to São Paulo, we stopped at a restaurant. I ordered a brandy and my father did not blink. He was reading a newspaper.

In São Paulo we took a room in a boarding house where no one visited us.

'We're going to Rio,' he told me, sitting on the bed and resting his one remaining arm on his legs.

In Rio, we went to an apartment on Avenida Atlântica. 'My friends' place,' he commented. But although the apartment was well furnished, it felt empty.

'I want to know,' I said to my father.

'That could be risky,' he replied.

And I turned off the television, ready to listen. He said no. It's still too soon. And I had already lost the ability to cry.

I tried to forget. My father put me in a school in Copacabana and I began to grow up just like so many adolescents in Rio. I screwed my schoolfriend Alfredinho's maid and sometimes, on the beach, I had to sit down quickly

because it often happened that I got hard just from someone
walking by. Then I used to pretend I was looking out to sea,
checking some surfer's performance. I didn't like to recognise
how much some things tormented me. Such as my father
disappearing again. I stayed alone in the apartment on
Avenida Atlântica without anyone finding out. I had got used
to the mystery of that apartment. Already I had no desire to
learn who it belonged to, why it felt so empty. The secret fed
my silence. And I needed that silence to keep on living there.
Ah – I forgot to say that my father had left a little money in
the safe. This money was enough for seven months. I didn't
spend much and tried not to think about what would happen
when it ran out. I knew that I was alone and my only source
of cash was running low, but I needed to preserve that free
and easy air that boys my age have, and faked my father's
signature without a scruple every time the school required
it.

I didn't give a damn about keeping the apartment clean.
It was truly filthy. But I was so rarely at home that I didn't
bother about the filth, the grimy sheets. I had good friends at
school, and two or three lady friends who gave me carte
blanche to go where I pleased.

But the money had run out and I was walking down
Avenida Nossa Senhora de Copacabana late one night when
I caught sight of a group of big guys standing on the corner
of Rua Barão de Ipanema, leaning on a car and rolling a joint.
When I walked past, they held it out to me. Want a toke? I
accepted. One of them nodded: Check it out, don't miss that
one, sweetheart! I looked where he'd pointed and saw a
Mercedes parked on the corner with a man of about 30
inside. Go on over, they urged me. And I went over.

'Want to get in?' the man asked.

I saw his game and remembered that I was skint.

'Three hundred, cash,' I said.

He opened the car door and said, 'Get in.' The car went
up by Avenida Niemeyer. There was no one about on the
hillside where the man stopped. A tape was playing, I think it

14

was a classical tune, and the man said he was from São Paulo. He offered me a cigarette, chewing gum, and began to take off my clothes. I asked for the cash first. He gave me three hundred-cruzeiro notes, brand-new and unfolded. And I was naked and the man started to get it on with me, biting me hard enough to leave marks, almost taking a chunk out of my mouth. I had a nice body and this got him all worked up, made him crazy. The tape had finished and all you could hear was a cricket.

'Let's go,' said the man, revving the car.

I'd come and had to clean myself up with a pair of swimming shorts.

The next day, my father came back, turned up at the door looking very thin, and with two teeth missing. I decided to tell him:

'Yesterday I had sex for money. I went with a man in exchange for three hundred cruzeiros.'

My father looked at me without surprise and told me to try making a different story out of my life. Then he sat down and spoke to the point:

'I've come to die. My death will be picked up by the papers. The police have it in for me; they've been chasing me for years. They'll find you but you don't make a single comment, say you know nothing about anything. Which is the truth.'

'What if they torture me?' I asked.

'You're a minor and they have to avoid a scandal.'

I went to the window thinking I was going to cry but only managed to stand there looking at the sea and thinking that I should do something urgently. I looked round and saw that my father was asleep. In fact, that wasn't really what I thought: I thought that he was already dead and I raced over to check his pulse. There was still life in him. *You must do something urgently*, my head was screaming at me. The thing is that I hadn't liked going with that man the night before, my father was dying and I hadn't a single *centavo*. How could I

15

make a living? Then I thought about handing my father over to the police, selling my story to the papers and getting a roof and food at an orphanage, or in some family's home. But no, I didn't do this because I liked my father and I wasn't interested in living in an orphanage or with another family, and it hurt to see my father lying there asleep on the sofa, looking so weak. Still I needed to speak to someone, to explain what was happening. Who?

I began to skip classes and spend my time walking on the beach, wondering what to do with my father, who was still at home, ugly and old, and asleep. And I hadn't managed to drum up even one more fucking *centavo*. Just as well I had a friend who worked as a Geneal vendor and who could sort me out with hotdogs. I would say: give it plenty of mustard, make this dog good and hot, and don't forget the ketchup. He obeyed as if he wanted the best for me. But I couldn't bring myself to tell him what was going on with me. I only pointed out women's arses to him, or the occasional scar on one of their bellies. It's a Caesarian, he informed me. I pretended I'd never heard about Caesarians, to add to his pleasure in teaching me what a Caesarian was. One day he asked me:

'How many brothers d'you have?'

Seven, I replied.

'Your father really goes for it, huh?'

I wondered what to reply; perhaps this was the moment to tell him everything, to admit that I needed help. But what could a Geneal hotdog seller do for me short of shopping us to the police? So I kept quiet and headed off.

When I got home I could hear at once that my father was dying. He wasn't fully conscious, was having convulsions and slurring his words as I watched. At that point the apartment smelled really bad, like something rotten. Only this time I didn't just look on, but tried to help the old man. I lifted his head up, tugged a pillow under it and tried to talk to him.

'What are you feeling?' I asked.

'I can't feel anything now,' he replied, with a frightful effort.

16

'Does it hurt?'

'There's no more pain.'

Now and then I would bring him a hotdog that my friend with the Geneal cart gave me, but my father rejected everything and spat bits of bread and sausage out of the corner of his mouth. One of these times, when I was cleaning the scraps of bread and sausage from his mouth with a dishcloth, the doorbell rang. The bell rang. I went to open the door, petrified, the dishcloth still in my hand. It was Alfredinho.

'The principal wants to know why you never show up at school,' he said.

I told him to come in and said that I'd been sick, with a throat infection, but that I'd come back to school tomorrow as I'd almost recovered. Alfredinho smelled the terrible smell in the house, I'm sure, but did his best not to show it.

When he sat down, I saw how shabby the sofa was and how Alfredinho was sitting rather carefully, as if the sofa were falling apart beneath his arse. But he covered up and acted as if he'd not seen anything wrong, not even the cockroach running down the wall to his right, or the sounds coming from my father, who was tossing around and moaning now and then in the bedroom next door. I took the armchair and sat there saying anything that entered my head in order to distract him from my father's noises, the cockroach on the wall, the sofa's collapse, the filth and stink of the apartment. I said that while I'd been ill I had stayed in bed all day reading dirty magazines, Danish dirty magazines, in fact, and did he know how I'd got hold of these magazines? I'd nicked them from my father's study where they'd been hidden in a drawer in his desk; I can't show you now because I've lent them to a friend, a bastard with a Geneal hotdog cart here on the beach. He showed a friend of his how he had a wank with the mag in his hand; there's a woman in it with her legs out like this and the camera takes her from right down here, right here, the fucker, the way guys take photos of women, her like this and the camera catching her right from this angle, isn't that worth a proper wank? The camera right up close and the lady butt-naked and her legs out like that, I swear, mate, you'll see, you'll see it one day, only right now I haven't got the mag. That's why I'm saying it's not a bad gig getting sick once in a while, spending the whole day lying in bed reading dirty mags, nobody to bug me about lessons and classwork, just me and my magazines; you should try it, mate, you'd have a good laugh being sick like this, with slutty mags, no one to hassle you, no one at all, mate, nobody.

Then I stopped talking and Alfredinho looked at me as if I were saying something frightening, sat there looking at me like a prick, like he didn't trust me, and I don't even know what went through his head when my father called out my name; it was the first time my father called me by my name and it even gave me a fright to hear him use my name, and I got up in a real panic because I didn't want anyone to know about my father, about my secret, about my life. I wanted Alfredinho to get out and not come back ever, so I stood up and said I had a few things to see to, and he backed away out the door, as if he were afraid of me, and me saying that I'd be at school tomorrow, you can tell the principal that I'll come and speak to her tomorrow, and my father called me again in his dying man's voice, my father was calling me by my name for the first time in my life and I said bye, see you tomorrow, and Alfredinho said bye, til tomorrow, and I was still there with the dishcloth in my hand. I closed the door fast because I couldn't take another second of Alfredinho there in my face not saying a word, and I ran to the bedroom and saw that my father's eyes had gone hard, looking at me, and I stayed standing in the bedroom doorway thinking I must do something urgently.

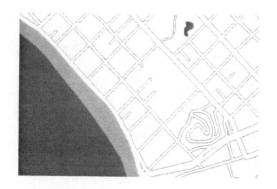

The Biggest Bridge in the World

Domingos Pellegrini

Translated by Jon S. Vincent

I USED TO have a pair of pliers like you wouldn't believe – yellow plastic handles that glowed in the dark – real German steel. I used them almost every day for eight years. They were with me at Ibitinga, Acaray, Osório Falls, Solteira Island and Capyvara Falls. If I had saved a yard of the copper wire every time I cut a line with those pliers, I'd have enough to last a lifetime. You know, when you lose a tool you've used a lot it's just like losing a finger.

I was working at Capyvara Falls. I was single, without a care in the world, life was a thing with no beginning and no end, and I thought working on dams was a big deal. All you had to do was sign up, always keep your hardhat on your head and your boots on your feet, and the rest the Company told you what to do. You finished one dam and they sent you to another, and life turned into a thing without beginning or end.

That day I had come back from the dam, taken a shower, and we were getting dressed for dinner – I was putting on my shirt and Fifty Volts had been combing his hair for about five minutes – he'd smear a smelly cream on his head and spend half an hour in front of the mirror, until a hank of hair came out in his comb, and then he'd pull it out and throw it on the floor. That's why dam workers' quarters always stink – one guy throws hair on the floor, another one spits, another leaves his wet towel on his cot, and the windows are always closed because there's always one crew sleeping and another on its way out and another coming in. Work on a dam never stops, day or night.

So there we were getting ready, about half an hour before supper, when a guy in a yellow boilersuit walks in, asks if I'm me and if Fifty Volts is him. Then he asked about the other electricians and Fifty Volts says he doesn't have any kids. The guy didn't get that and asked if they hadn't said where they were going before they left, and Fifty Volts came back and said they didn't ask for his permission when they went out. Then the guy looked at Fifty Volts and said OK, buddy, that's fine, I'll fix you up with a nice mule so you can have a good time. Fifty Volts was about to argue some more but the guy said the earlier we found the others the earlier we'd get going.

Then Fifty Volts asked where the party was going to be, and the guy answered, serious: in Rio de Janeiro, pal. I looked out the door and saw a yellow van with Rio plates, turned to Fifty Volts and told him the guy wasn't kidding. Then another guy in a yellow boilersuit came in with the three electricians who'd left, pulled a piece of paper out of his pocket, and called Fifty Volts and my names and asked the other guy: Where are these two?

I saw that the paper was Company paper, and I was already pulling off my clothes and putting on my work clothes, but Fifty Volts still wanted to argue with them, because he had just come off a sixteen-hour shift, hadn't eaten, and what's all the hurry and so forth, but the men just said: Look, buddy, if you don't get ready we'll leave you, and you can take care of yourself – but by then Fifty Volts had already started changing.

Keep your good clothes on, pal – one of the guys said, and the other one: On the way we'll stop and pick up some chicks. Then it only took Fifty Volts a minute to get his gear together, all five of us got in the van, and the two guys got in front. We stopped at the Company office and a nice-looking secretary came out with some papers for us to sign right there inside the van. Everybody signed, and there was hardly time to give the pen back because the van took off in a big cloud of dust, and then we noticed that the back of the van was padded, just like a bed but with a canvas cover – and in the corner were two styrofoam boxes.

Fifty Volts took the lid off one of the boxes, and the whole thing was full of canned beer and crushed ice, and in the middle a bottle of brandy. In the other cooler, more beer and a litre of yellow rum. Then one of the guys in front looked back, knocked on the glass so everybody would look at him, and signaled by putting his thumb in his mouth, meaning we could drink all we wanted.

About an hour later they stopped at a restaurant, and we all got out as well as we could and the guys said: You can eat all you want because it's on the house. We went in and started to chow down – ribs, roast beef, chicken, steak – I ate so much I was sick. It occurred to me to ask what sodding dam it was that we were going to wire, but the topic by then was women and we took off in the van again drinking beer with brandy, in that wild mood you get when you're going to get laid, and in less than a hundred metres the van stopped.

The house had five women, just right. Fifty Volts got stuck with a fat redhead, and I got a little brunette with a nice face, hard tits, and a tight belly, but within a minute I could tell she was an icecube. I stuck my hand in her and it was just like sticking your hand in a sofa, nothing but stuffing; and there was the fat one with Fifty Volts by her, and she was so cranked up you'd think she had a hot coal in her.

Everybody was playing grab-ass, and every once in a while one of the chicks would get up to get more beer or change the record, and the two guys in yellow boilersuits just hung around outside, like watchdogs. Finally one couple went to the bedroom, then another, and me there with that icecube, and Fifty Volts with the fat one on his lap licking his ear and his neck, and the sofa felt like a boat on rough water, bouncing back and forth, and I couldn't figure out why Fifty Volts hadn't headed for the room yet. And me with my chick, with her hand on my knee like it was an ashtray. When I said things to her, she just answered yes or no.

Then I leaned over to fill my glass and noticed that Fifty Volts had his hand on my little brunette's other knee. So I reached back and grabbed the fat one's ear so she could see but not him, and I started sticking it in and going around her ear with my finger, and she kept looking at me all fired up, wiggling her tongue around at me. So I told Fifty Volts to go outside with me and take a leak, showed him how it was a starry night and asked him if he wanted to trade. We went back in and I sat down with the fat one and he went over to the brunette, poor guy. For me, it was just a matter of sitting down, steadying the boat a minute and heading for the bedroom.

The fat girl started taking her clothes off standing on the bed, and I was afraid the frame would break, but she kept taking things off and hopping around. She was fat but had good balance, because when she took her knickers off she stood on one foot and then on the other one, and I realized then that she was a real redhead, even down there. She only had a black bra left on, a tiny little thing that was too tight on her, so when she took it off her tits seemed to jump out. Then she did a whole turn, not too graceful, to show that she was really fat but wasn't ashamed of being fat. Then she faced me again, opened her legs, and asked if I thought she was too fat, and I said she was as good as she was heavy, and then I got up and stood on the bed, too, almost naked.

So she grabbed me and pulled me down, and the bedframe broke and she kept squeezing me between her legs and saying Skinny Baby, Skinny Baby, and I was lost in that mass of her. Then she sat on me, just as they knocked on the door: Time to go, pal.

I was the last one. When I went outside, Fifty Volts and the others were already in the van, so I just got in and off we went. The fat girl came to the window with a towel around her and waved, and I started thinking: These guys were even going the price of a girl for us — in exchange for what? The van was hitting the curves at 60 miles an hour. All of a sudden, after wasting all that time, they were in a hurry.

It started to rain pitchforks and the van was still cooking along at over 70. The others went to sleep, all rolled up together with their knees against each others' heads and their elbows against each others' necks. I spent the night wide awake. About dawn I started dozing off and Fifty Volts wakes up and says: You should have gotten some sleep, buddy. I asked him if he'd been screwing my mother to be giving me advice like a father, but he kept on. That I should have gotten some sleep. That it was going to be rough. They had orders to fill us up with booze, let us all get laid, and eat meat until we were stuffed. All that so later nobody would demand time off.

With the sky turning all red and the sun coming up I thought Fifty Volts was exaggerating, and I said that nobody dies from working too hard on a Sunday. Then he said: I don't know. I don't think we're going to get off that bridge until either the job or us is done.

The men stopped for a good breakfast, with bread, cheese, butter, honey, milk and crackers, and I thought again that Fifty Volts was exaggerating.

I saw the statue of Christ the Redeemer and a minute later the van stopped. It was the bridge.

The bridge is so big that from one end of it you can't see the other. They told me later that it's the biggest one in the world, but I guessed that the minute I saw it — the biggest bridge in the world.

The inauguration was a month away, and the whole place was crawling with workmen from top to bottom. You were always running into engineers, carpenters, hod carriers, specialists like me, supervisors, assistant supervisors, sub-supervisors, and every other kind of visor they've ever invented, guards, inspectors, inspectors' assistants, or security chiefs jumping on somebody for taking off his helmet. And visitors. Once in a while a visitor would show up in a coat and tie with a brand new hardhat on, falling all over everything and asking questions. One came up to me one day and asked if I wasn't proud to be working on the biggest bridge in the world. And I said: I didn't know it was the biggest bridge in the world, man, to me it's just a bridge. But he insisted: Well, I want you to know that it is the biggest bridge in the world, and to work on it is a privilege for all of us. So I asked: Us who? What kind of work do you do around here?

Then all hell broke loose: who said what, what did you say, things like that. But later nobody bothered me because one electrician less in a place like that would make a lot of difference. There was work to do, not to do, to do wrong; there was more work than there were people, but if they brought more people there wouldn't have been room for them on the bridge. When we arrived the electrical system was barely started. We worked night and day on an emergency schedule, setting up one portable generator here and another there, light sockets all over the place, a lot of it with bare wire and jerrybuilt fittings. Every one of those workers got more shocks in a day than a normal person does in a lifetime.

And that was what they handed to us to straighten out, a mountain of wires that came in one way and went out another, nobody knew how or why; a powerhouse connected to everything but without any controls. It was like a cow with two hundred tits, with milk coming out of one and coffee out the next. And overloads all the time, because part of the power was 110 and part 220, Niterói on one side and Rio on the other, and in the middle about twenty electricians working all night without sleep to make it work.

Every day a new electrician showed up, but the work continued without a break. First we had to set up a central power system, install the distribution boxes, and wire in a substation for each section of the bridge. On that part we chin-wagged more than we worked because the ones looking after that were a big blond engineer and his men. Then we got to the wiring itself, laying conduit, connecting cables, laying out the circuits for the topside lights, and installing the interior lighting – because the bridge has sleeping quarters, a control station, and a lab, all built-in.

And we worked by the kilometre. So many kilometres of wire here, so many kilometres of cable there. And it was day and night, night and day. Triple overtime, with everybody putting in eighteen, twenty, twenty-four hours with pliers in your hand, and the man constantly hollering in your ear: Let's see some hustle, boys, let's see some hustle, because we only have three weeks. Let's see some hustle because we only have two weeks. One of the guys who worked with me, Arnold, fell asleep on his face on the seventh day, with his mouth right next to the end of a high tension cable. He left the bridge and went straight to the hospital and never came back. I think he was fired, but I don't know. An apprentice from Paraíba used to sing all the time while he worked. I don't know what the hell his name was, but he fell four metres onto a slab of concrete and one of the steel reinforcing rods in the concrete went six inches into his thigh and they carried him off bleeding like a pig. But he came back three days before the inauguration, hobbling like an old rooster.

And the man hollering in your ear: Let's see some hustle, men, because we only have a week. A workman went over a high-tension cable on the ground, pushing a wheelbarrow full of cement. He went over it twice, but the third time he hit the cable splice with the wheel, and I heard a tremendous bang and looked just in time to see him go up in the air like somebody had kicked him. He came down with his clothes all scorched and his boots ended up ten metres away. Then

27

there was a big hassle about who had left a live cable lying around on the ground like that, how can you do a thing like that, and so on, and they rolled the dead man up in a blanket and let's see some hustle, we only have a week left, men.

One day I climbed a pole, where I could see the whole bridge from one end to the other. There must have been two or three thousand men, I don't know, but more than on any dam I ever saw. Just like an anthill when you step on it and stir it up. And everybody mad, with workmen kicking each other and running into each other because they never stopped yelling there's only a week left, only six days.

A kid with a yellow boilersuit came by every couple of hours with hot coffee in paper cups, and we drank it and kept spitting black saliva all the time. When you don't sleep for a long time, you start salivating, did you ever notice? Wherever you saw black spit on the ground you knew the guy had worked twenty-four or thirty hours without sleep. Workmen slept under tarps, on cots, on the floor, right next to somebody hammering. And all night long the electric saws kept cutting, the cement mixers kept going, and the trucks kept dumping stuff. Some guys you had to wake up with a bucket of water, and they'd start walking round, half asleep, asking people what needed doing. If somebody had said jump off the bridge they would have done it. The ocean was everywhere you looked, and the sun was beating down up on top and we were frying. Even in the open air it was like being in a tunnel, because you never had time to look up, you never had time to spit and see it hit the ground.

You'd lay down more dead than alive but you couldn't close your eyes until your body started to relax. After about two hours you'd fall asleep and wake up to hear: only five more days, people, five days! – and it seemed like you had only slept five minutes because your joints were coming apart, your head was swimming, your eyes were dry and full of a kind of sand you couldn't wash out and there came the kid with the coffee. You looked at your watch – you always got eight hours off, but minus the time wasted trying to get to sleep, minus the time to take a bath before, shave, and so on, it ended up less than five hours of sleep. Fifty Volts let his beard grow.

Then all the electricians stopped taking showers. The last week we reeked. Once in a while I'd hear a slap – it was somebody hitting himself in the face to wake up. I pinched my ear or sometimes my nipple, just to be sure I was alive, because sometimes it all seemed like a dream. Lack of sleep makes you dizzy right down to your bones.

The food for electricians came on aluminium trays with pressure lids, so you could just pop the lid and eat wherever you were. The third time I took off the lid and saw feijoada,[5] I realized it was Saturday and next day would be Sunday. It would be my third Sunday in a row without a break. Then I turned to Fifty Volts and said: Want to know something, buddy? I've had it.

The kid with the coffee came by and I told him to stick his coffee up his arse and started out looking for the foreman. Fifty Volts went along. I didn't even have to say anything; he guessed I was going to ask for my pay and get off the bridge, go find a hotel room and sleep, because all I could think of was a bed. Fifty Volts had been saving up to go back to his part of the country and buy a bar, so I thought he had come along just out of curiosity, but right there in front of the foreman he asked for his pay too. I'm not some kind of an animal to work without rest, he said, and the foreman agreed but said that he couldn't do anything, that he could hardly see himself but there was nothing he could do, we'd have to talk to the chief of the electric section.

We talked to the section chief, then to an engineer, then to a supervisor who sent for an engineer from our Company. These men are from your Company, engineer, he said, and they are asking for their pay. The Company is deeply invested in this bridge, men, the engineer said. You can't leave just like

5. A bean stew with beef and pork.

that. There was a circular saw cutting timbers nearby, so we had to talk when the saw stopped and it started getting on our nerves.

I said we had the right to leave whenever we wanted to, and that was that. Then some character with a suit but no tie showed up and the engineer kept talking and the saw kept cutting. When he finished Fifty Volts waited for the saw to stop and said that we weren't animals to be working like that, and the supervisor said that if the problem was needing a woman he'd see what he could do about it. Then the engineer said that there were over twenty companies working on the bridge, most of them at a déficit, because it had become a question of honor. We had to finish the bridge, and our Company would never forget our work there on the bridge, a source of national pride. The supervisor asked if the food wasn't up to snuff, if we wanted more coffee on the job, and all I said was no, all I wanted to do was get my money and get away from there, and Fifty Volts kept saying he wasn't an animal to be working like that. The guy in the suit put his hand on his belt and his jacket opened in front and you could see a .38 sticking out.

Then, when the saw stopped the guy with the .38 looked right at me and said: Look, buddy, if you want cash in your hand you can have it right now, but you're going to stay on the job because the only other way you're going to get off this bridge is dead. The engineer said that the Company had a bonus for us so it would be better for us to stay on voluntarily, so as not to betray the Company's confidence in us. Then Fifty Volts said: Right, we'll rest a while and go back to work in better spirits. But the guy with the .38 thought it would be better for us to show our good faith by going straight back to work, so I threw a bucket of water on my head and went back.

For an electrician to work wet is the same as for a fireman to work naked – you're asking for trouble. But it was the only way. It was like the end of the world – the men were staggering, and visitors came by the batch asking if everything was going OK, if everything was all right, if we were in good spirits. And now visitors didn't wear hardhats any more because the inauguration was so near. We just answered yes, Sir, yes, Sir. Anything they asked we answered yessir like a bunch of ghosts. If they had said it was the biggest bridge in the world we would have answered yessir because I at least couldn't even hear any more and my hands worked while my head slept. The calluses on my hands started peeling because there was no time for new skin to form. At night I'd look at Rio and then at Niterói, and I kept asking why do the people over there need to come over here and the ones over here need to go over there?

Then painters started showing up everywhere you looked, and we started kicking into cans of paint, traffic signs, brackets, and screws to put the signs up with. An order came down to concentrate ten electricians on the external lighting of the bridge, where no work at all had been done yet. We put up a beautifully disguised emergency light system, really pretty. Anybody who saw it would say it was wonderful. It looked like a Christmas tree. But if a strong wind had hit it, it would have gone right in the drink.

One day a general announcement was made that the next day was the inauguration, and I fell in bed with all my clothes on with itches on my head and all over my body from not having bathed and a callus on my forehead from using the hardhat so much. Then a counter-order came for us not to stop work or part of the bridge would still be dark. We couldn't allow it to happen. It was shameful, let's go men, this bridge is the pride of Brazil, and so on, and we had to climb up there ourselves and put in the lights. All night long balancing yourself ten metres up, with the wind coming by and the dark ocean, and it was enough to make you want to jump and go down, down. It made you dizzy, it made you sorry to be an electrician and mad at whoever invented electricity.

I'd never taken pills to stay awake, but that night everybody took them. Fifty Volts said: Here, buddy, swallow this because this is the last round and tomorrow you can sleep until your arse falls off. I took them with coffee, three little pills the same colour as the hardhats, yellow, and then I climbed a pole and just stared at the others in their yellow hardhats up there in the dark, every one just like one of those pills mired in coffee. I remember staying a long time staring at them, until somebody nudged me and I worked right through until in the morning.

There was a band playing someplace when they put us in the vans – nine o'clock in the morning and 40 electricians with their eyes bugged out, all with black circles under them like they'd been punched. Fifty Volts stuck his finger in his ear and was surprised when he pulled out a black ball. I took off my boot and nobody could stand the smell, so I had to stick my feet out the window of the van to air them out. They took us to a beach, and everybody ran down to the water with their pants rolled up or just in their shorts with a bar of soap, every one of them with more beard than the next guy. It was when I started taking my clothes off that I realized the pliers were missing from my belt.

I had never been in the ocean in my life, and I still haven't. I stayed in the van hunting around for the pliers, and when the others came back and changed I was still stinking.

At 11 in the morning we got out at a restaurant by the beach. Feijoada. I don't know whether it was Saturday or not, but they had feijoada – with rum and lemon, beer, and more feijoada. When the rum hit my head the tiredness turned into dumb happiness, and I had such a buzz I forgot all about sleep and the pliers and the filth. There were workers there who didn't know the others' names, and one guy who sang xaxado[6] and baiao[7] and stuff like that, and the lame guy from Paraíba danced along to the music, stomping out the beat right to the rhythm. Fifty Volts delivered a speech saying that the biggest short circuit in the world was going to happen on that bridge, and I gave a speech too but I don't remember what about. I do remember that at one point the owner of the restaurant came over and asked us to stop singing 'Marvelous City', and Fifty Volts said we'd only stop if it was to eat some more nice hot feijoada. And more came, bowl after steaming bowl of it, with dried beef, pig's feet, pork ears, sausages, ribs, all the stuff that a decent feijoada has to have, and they served it with greens and manioc flour and oranges that were already peeled – you just ate one and shovelled down some more feijoada.

Then the numbness hit us. The coffee came but nobody there could even stand to look at it – forty electricians at a long table, all in the pits, belching like a bunch of toads and picking their teeth for orange fibres. To tell the truth I don't know where I slept, but I woke up the next day at four in the afternoon in a room with vomit all over the floor. I took a shower, had dinner in a dining hall with yellow-tiled walls and went back to sleep. The next day they put us in another van, only this time it wasn't padded. It occurred to me to stop by the bridge and find the pliers and Fifty Volts asked if I was crazy. He had heard on the radio that who knows how many thousands of cars passed over the bridge every day, and here was me wanting to look for some pliers.

To this day Fifty Volts talks about working on the bridge, but I don't. He even says that, some day, he's going to go to Rio to see the bridge all lit up, but I've already seen it, the other day in a magazine.

---

6. A popular dance created in the Sertão of Pernambuco state, often practiced to commemorate victory in battle.
7. A northeastern rhythmic formula, usually played with a zabumba, a flat, double-headed bass drum.

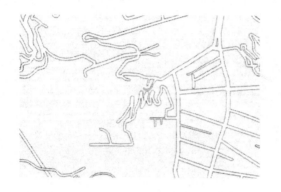

Song of Songs

Nei Lopes

Translated by Amanda Hopkinson

We have a little sister and her breasts are still not grown.
What shall we do for our little sister on the day she is spoken
for?
　　Song of Songs 8:8

GILBERTO BRODSTEIN PARKS his car, checks the doors are
properly locked, puts the key back on its gold key ring, and
crosses the road crowded with people. He looks around him
until he spots his float, with the camel that bears the Queen
of Sheba on her legendary journey.

This legend, as interpreted by the samba parade, relates
how one day, some 950 years before Christ, the Sovereign
Ruler of the Kingdom of Sheba – located in the south of
Arabia but under strong influence from the adjacent lands of
Ethiopia – decided to uncover the nature of the celebrated
treasures of Solomon, King of Israel, by putting his legendary
wisdom to the test. Arriving at Jerusalem laden with gifts for
the ruler, the black Queen set Solomon a series of riddles,
that he elucidated with calm ease. Even while she was
becoming enchanted by the wisdom of Solomon, Queen
Belkiss charmed him in return with her beauty, awakening in
him a desire for the wealth and luxury she displayed. After an
intense period of romance and sensuality, a royal dynasty was
born of their union…..or at least, that's the way their version
of the story goes, one that, between ourselves, did nothing
whatsoever to please our main character.

Gilberto is president of the University Samba School, the 'Professor of Samba' as the logo says. Members of the School are drawn from the business and management sector, liberal professionals like himself, nearly all of them bearing their graduation ring on their finger and living in comfort on the city side of the tunnel, well away from the hillside *favela* where the samba school was founded. But Gilberto is a womanising, party-loving Bohemian, and Carnival is not something to be overlooked. All the less so nowadays, when a samba school is a sound, attractive and inexpensive form of entertainment.

The son of a shopkeeper on the Rua do Catete, and a good businessman with a long track record as the resident manager of properties on the Botafogo street called Voluntários da Pátria, Gilberto became known as 'Beto Botafogo', not only after his neighbourhood but also out of loyalty to his football team. He soon rose to become president of the local Sector, and modernised the University Samba School, introducing credit card payments for monthly bills, and ordering up new costumes and finery on an industrial scale.

In the past, one block of a samba school consisted in a half-dozen barefoot kids who gathered on a street corner or in a cheap bar and decided to build a float for the Carnival parade. The names they gave their Schools always boasted either of aristocracy or intrepidity: The Barons' Block; The Impossibles; the Bastions; the Court; the Magnates... But every one of the Carnival costumes, since they were all created at home on the basis of a rough pattern – a kind of blueprint – was transferred onto umpteen tissue paper copies, before being distributed to all the local seamstresses. Each costume then emerged in a different version, with only the faintest and most primitive features of the original. When the groups didn't meet up on the street corner, they formed inside the houses themselves. That was where relatives, friends, work colleagues met up – and where the final outcome, in terms of the cut and fit of the costumes, generally left something to be desired.

At that time, one could only become director of a samba school through being a brave and fearless individual, someone who kept a sharp knife in a back pocket. In the Brazil of today, an orderly and progressive country since the 1970s, samba school directors tend to be well-bred, with the good manners to represent their schools at the highest levels of society, to those in government and municipal office, and even overseas. It is compulsory for such individuals to come with clean references; no kind of police record; and no aberration whatsoever in their own official documents, so that whenever necessary they could obtain a safe-conduct, or a passport to undertake this or that type of mission.

For example, Beto Botafogo, is trained in management. And he goes in person to obtain supplies from São Paulo. There, on the basis of the subject given him for that year's Carnival, he places the order for the costumes, and on the basis of the pattern he provides, he opens the bidding for a contract. Thanks to such professionalism, he is by now quite at ease.

There are still some four hours to go before the parade begins. But Beto Botafogo, as School president, has to assemble all the component parts of his Section, line them up in their correct positions (behind the float bearing the Queen of Sheba), resolve any outstanding problems, and take charge of his block, before sounding the war cry and setting off the battery of fire crackers that hail the start of Carnival.

Thirty-five years old and born under the Zodiac sign of Leo, Beto Botafogo is married to Marilia, a French teacher, practising Catholic and fierce opponent of Carnival. Marilia spends its three days of celebration reading her books and reciting her devotions. In all the years of their marriage, she has only once joined the carnival block. And then she did not appreciate the sweaty crowds – or the stench of fatty meat on the street barbecues littered with plastic cups – one little bit.

Meanwhile Beto, notwithstanding his chain of office and his wristwatch glittering beneath the lights, arrives in the midst of the crowd wearing on the fourth finger of his left hand the signet ring that is the seal of his authority. And it is from the heights of his position of superiority that he observes the *mulatta* girl, touching up her make-up as she chats to a friend.

Edna da Silva is twenty years old and earns a minimal wage working in a nail bar. She lives in a *favela* on the Morro mountainside. And, since she doesn't have the money to buy a costume, she joins the popular block known as the Comunidade.

All the same, without money and with few other resources with which to make her costume, Edna is beautiful. Naturally beautiful. And she is fully aware of her budding curves, albeit still semi-adolescent, barely hinted at by her outfit; of her shiny skin as brown as chocolate; of her smile and her chatter able to light up an entire avenue.

Beto Botafogo is in ecstasy. *Take good note / that every word she speaks / lights up the room more than a spotlight.* This samba song from his childhood pops into his head. So Beto offers her a swig of the whisky he is sipping.

'Thank-you! But I only drink beer…'

Like something produced by an Arabian djinn, or a conjuror from a box of tricks, a can of beer appears, ridiculously cold, covered in moisture, from an insulated bag concealed in the majestic allegorical float of the Queen of Sheba.

'The Comunidade?'

'Yes of course? That's my place…'

'Next year you could go out on the float…'

'And the money for that? I'm a manicurist, my angel!'

'Why do you think that's a problem?'

'Perhaps it isn't for you…'

'Haven't you noticed how pretty you are?'

'Thank you.'

'You look like the Queen of Sheba.'

'Get over it!'

'You are as pretty as the *Cidade Maravilhosa* – our City of Rio – as enchanting as Petropolis, and as impressive as both those cities put together!'

'Blimey! How romantic you are! I'm all of that?'

'Something also tells me that you will be my queen.'

And so it came to pass. Three years on, with a Carnival theme on 'The Dawn of the Gods Ile Oyo and Ile Ife', you could behold little Edna go out as a key figure in the parade, personifying Moremi, Orania's wife, who won her laurels in the war of the Ife people against the Igbo people, according to the text assigned to that year's Carnival parade – bestowing beauty, generosity and sensuality from on high upon her allegorical float. A whole float to herself, only a tiny bit smaller than Soraya's. But one day, who knows...?

Soraya is the first lady of the School. The daughter of a Portuguese greengrocer, she had begun her career parading on foot. Then she rose to be queen of the percussionists, took the *mulatta*'s part in the float displays, directed spectacles, acted as a godmother to the section dedicated to composers, and went out in more and more prominent roles. She took charge of publicity for the School management and, conquered the already rickety but ever-hopeful heart of the magnanimous Senhor Albano, to ascend the dais of the lead allegorical float.

Back at home Marilia watches television and sees the apotheosis of her newly shattered marriage. Beto Botafogo, by now an influential member of the board of directors, barks his orders with feigned ill temper and studied stress. But, from deep inside his three-piece white linen suit, the director is enjoying the success of his dark little *morena*. Marilia switches the TV channel. And she pauses it to watch a documentary on monastic life in the mountains of Ethiopia.

★   ★   ★

A separation by mutual consent soon comes through. It doesn't cause too much fuss, since only the two of them are involved. None the less, Marilia demands their house in Teresópolis, the one she had inherited from her father; their flats in the downtown Darke condominium; the building lots they own in Itaipuaçu, and the car. But Beto behaves like a sound businessman in contenting himself with the flat in Voluntarios, since he knows that soon, very soon, he will obtain much more.

From the splendid maturity of her blossoming 28 years, little Edna exits from the Morro of the *favelas* in triumph, bringing with her the daughter she had at the age of seventeen, to go and settle in Botafogo. The old neighbourhood is split: one half thinks she has just landed in luck, and so is now living out a fairy tale; others prophecy that none of this will turn out well. After all, the 'white director' is rising high, moving on from his old company in order to become involved in Senhor Albano's business ventures. It is he who now represents the Association's samba school, at whose meetings he is on a short fuse, constantly complains, even thumps the table.

Belkiss – whose name was lifted from a magazine that appeared one day in the nail bar – is now just twelve years old and a sight to be seen. That was how she came to join the file of the 'Black Gods, from Egypt to Infinity', with groups of young *mirins,* children already training to become *passistas*, expert dancers, all sponsored by Joãozinho's Manicure Parlour. And how that young girl can samba! What nails, what determination and grace she exhibits, duly approved by the Youth Jury! She showily flaunts her way along the parade ground of the Avenue, displaying an instinctively precise sense of spectacle, an innate dancer's talent, and an extraordinary sensuality. A sensuality she exerts even inside the home, as you can see from the following:

'What do you mean by this, girl! Behave yourself and cover yourself up! Get some clothes on.' Beto is plainly shaken, his blood is boiling in his veins, being faced with so much beauty enclosed in nothing more than a bra and knickers.

'I came to give you a surprise! I made the most out of Mum not being here...'

'But... this is madness...'

'Everyone tells me you are really knowledgeable, and a total expert,' Bebel says and sits down on the edge of the bed.

'Bebel... you are my daughter...'

'Hmmm... silly billy! Do you really think I don't notice the way you look at me?'

'And...'

'So what? Mum will only be back late tonight, stupid Bobo!'

'Come here...'

'No! Waait.... First of all, you need to reply to three questions from me.'

'Go on... go on, ask away then, my love...'

'Taaake your hand off! At once! Answer, I tell you! When a woman lies down, where does she lay her hand?'

'Now...'

'You don't know, do you? You just don't know,' Bebel laughs. 'It lies on her wrist, stupid Bobo!'

'Bebel, my love...'

'Noooo...! I've still got two more questions. Go on, answer me! What spheres am I talking about: the male of the species gets eaten and the female of the species rolls over...'

'My angel, my little love...'

'You don't know, I've got you! The spheres are, "the bun and the ball",[8] Senhor Idiot!'

'Little Bebel, please don't play games with me...'

'Now to the very last question! So far, you are neither knowing nor experienced, still less the expert? Let's go for it, then! Last question. What is it that you put on the table, you divide and share, but never eat?'

Beto Botafogo knew the answer to this one, but other matters were uppermost in his mind just at that moment.

'Let me in, my darling, my love, my little dove with perfect wings. My head is damp with evening mist. And my

8. *O bolo* (masculine) *e a bola* (feminine).

hair is wet with dew,' Beto Botafogo was declaiming incoherently. And Bebel re-incorporated Belkiss in an equally inappropriate declamation, one that could only have occurred in the mind of a merry-maker just out of samba school:

'"*May your lips cover me all over with kisses!*" Your love tastes sweeter than a pineapple ice-cream sundae! Your odour is so attractive to me. Go on! Take me with you! Ah, be my king! Go on! Go! I am your *mulatta* and I am gorgeous! Go on! I am as black as the *favela*'s open sewers! It is love... love mee... let me diiie... Aaaahhh...'

★   ★   ★

Poor Edna! She suspected nothing at all. Since now her only activities are exclusively Carnival related, she starts to acquire new hobbies. She only wakes up to greet the day at eleven o'clock... and now has at her disposal an incredible variety of breads, buns, sweets and biscuits... she considers that a Sunday without a gigantic dish of macaroni is like love without a kiss on the mouth...

Beto seeks to give her some sound advice:

'You are turning into a whale, don't you try to deny it! One of these days, you'll end up in the School of the Baianas, those women from the Northeast who are the largest in the whole of Brazil!'

But Dona Edna pretends she can neither hear nor understand. Then she adds to her daily afternoon routine a cup of Coca-Cola, along with a slice of pizza margarita, not to mention another cake stuffed with cream, while she sits in her armchair keeping her eyes firmly glued to the television.

Four carnivals later, in the float entitled 'Legends and Mysteries from the Valley of the Kings: from Thebes to Tupinambás', Bebel finally takes the Avenue leading through the Sambadrome by storm. She appears as Semenkhare, the name under which the beautiful and legendary Nefertiti reigned following the death of the Pharoah Akhenaten, who as well as being her husband was also first of all not as History tells us, her cousin, but neither more nor less than her father. It was one of those incestuous relationships so common in Ancient Egypt – as the carnival parade relates in its script, more in search of sensationalism than historical facts.

The School manages to achieve only seventh place. This is mainly as a result of the absurdity of its theme, based on a supposed and improbable arrival of Egyptian navigators on the shores of a Brazil, 1200 years BC, confusing Indians with pharaohs. In the end, however, the extravagance and sumptuousness of the girl's appearance impressed and ruled supreme. From the top of her pyramid, Belkiss Conceicao da Silva, our very own Bebel, succeeded in captivating Greeks and Trojans alike, in other words the whole world. Emotions ran so high that things went badly for Dona Edna, wretched and fatter than a pig (these were Beto Botafogo's words), cholesterol and triglycerines way over the limit, on her procession down the Avenue. Next day the newspapers blazed portraits of her on her litter, her mouth half-twisted, eyes wild, one arm dangling, and the left pocket of her blazer still embroidered with a badge reading: *Women's Section*.

* * *

Certain esoteric circles attributed the events of 1988 to the curse of the Pharoah. Or to the Zombie of Palmares, to whom everyone was paying homage that year. Everyone, that is, apart from Senhor Albano's School, who had gone for a different theme. From that Carnival onwards Dona Edna, sorely afflicted by her vascular 'accident', otherwise known as a 'heart attack', led a dog's life, prematurely aged by at least forty years.

Bebel, for her part, has no complaints. She lacks for nothing at all, and everything in her life runs fabulously well now that 'White Man', as she calls Beto Botafogo, is the executive president of the School (with Senhor Albano as the honorary president). White Man's businesses prosper so that his name has become synonymous with 'respect' both in the city centre and up in the *favelas*. His School wins the hat trick, the championship three times over, thereby fulfilling numerous predictions on the part of the special interest Carnival media.

'I wish to dedicate this trophy to my mother, who unfortunately cannot be here, but who taught me all I know. And I also dedicate it to the famous photographer Menelek, my fiancé, whom you all know. It was he who put me on the cover of *Play Time* magazine. And it was thanks to that front cover that, ever since, my talent has come to be recognised by all...'

Bebel is so overcome with emotion that she cannot complete her speech.

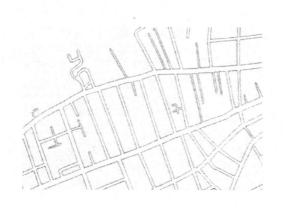

Lucky was Sandra

Luiz Ruffato

Translated by Jethro Soutar

SANDRA WAS LUCKY: having been baptised in the salt waters
of Bica and Engenhoca, her feet never forgot their way back
to Rio de Janeiro. Raised on Ilha do Governador, in the
Morro do Dendê *favela*, overlooking the Cacuia beaches, she
continued to act like a Carioca after being dumped in the
Cataguases foothills in early adolescence. She affected the
melodious hiss of the accent, the streetwise gestures of 'big
city people', and hated waking up every morning in a stuffy
box-house in dead-end Ana Carrara. She soon gave up
studying, much to the disappointment of her mother and
Zezé, her older brother, the family's sole breadwinner since
the death of their father. The family that now only existed in
a photograph, taken one long-ago seventh of September
(how old was I? five? six?) – ten faces, unrecognisable and
forever apart, three lads (Junim, still having to be held), six
idiot females, and her, Sandra, the only one with any brains:
she was nobody's fool. Nádia and Evelina, vanished off the
face of the earth; Cláudia, devout, her life surrendered to
worship, her husband and her gang of brats; Maura, depressed
singleton; Beatriz, dead... their mother, dead... a bedraggled
bunch of empty-headed women.

But back then... Back then Sandra learned she was
different. Dona Diana, Doctor Manoel Prata's wife, could
have chosen Maura, already fully eighteen years old, but she
took a shine to Sandra, not yet sixteen, paying her no end of

compliments. *Dona Nazaré, your daughter's smart, but, pardon me senhora, she has so little future here, stuck in Cataguases. Why don't you give the poor little thing a chance?* said Dona Diana, talking Sandra up, filling her head with dreams. She tried twice, three times more, pulling up in front of the house, leaving the engine running on her Escort, unyielding before Sandra's mother's insistence, *Why don't you come inside? have a coffee? a glass of water?* extremely polite behind her dark glasses, *No, Dona Nazaré, thank you very much, but I'm in a bit of a rush, some other time,* the nice smell of rich people, fresh out of the shower, suspicious of the dusty ground, the channels of dirty water, the mosquitoes, the drunken bums festering in the hot sun. And Sandra defied her mother, *I'm going!* and sniped at Zezé, *You don't control me!* and insulted Maura, *Retard!* and gathered her clothes and put them in a leather bag and took off.

A princess, riding in the front seat of the Volkswagen Santana – 'Prefeitura Municipal de Cataguases' emblazoned down the side – she got out at Praia de Botafogo, where Dona Diana, impervious to the blinding Sunday sun, presented her to *My treasures: Rafael,* taking his university entrance exam, *Samuel,* future qualified lawyer, *Marcela,* almost a doctor. *And here's your little hideaway!,* the tiny maid's quarters, dark and musty, bed and wardrobe crammed in. Marcela, barely there, stuck for days on end at the Hospital do Fundão, requiring only for her clothes to be immaculately white and the fridge to be well-stocked. Samuel, disgusting, clothes scattered about the apartment, whining, bullying, arrogant, unfriendly, cynical, taxing. And Rafael, gentle, lazy, television on, crap to eat. She soon tired of it all.

Five months of barely setting foot outside, trapped in her routine: tidy up, clean, cook, wash, iron, a blocked view of the dirty back of the building opposite, brief visits to the corner shop in emergencies, bulk deliveries brought in a Cataguases civil service car the first Thursday of every month, rice, black beans, kidney beans, Minas cheese, cottage cheese, tins of meat in pork fat, oil, salt, glass jars of fruit compotes. Until she found out Samuel smoked spliffs, worked out Marcela slept at her boyfriend's student halls, realised Rafael stalked her, like a nervous goat. *If you tell on me, I'll kill you!* snarled Samuel, terrified – and thus she was excused Friday nights. *Sandrinha, this is our little secret, okay?* whispered Marcela, stressed – and she won Saturdays. Flirtatious, she manipulated Rafael – and seized Sundays.

They were dizzy times. She'd escape on Friday night and make for Zona Norte – Abolição, Madureira, Ramos, Oswaldo Cruz – wherever the party was, and return Sunday evening, in the small hours, Monday morning, happily wrecked. And they'd complain, *Sandra, the place is a tip!* and she'd challenge them, *Get me sacked then, huh!* and retire to her 'little hideaway', under the lustful gaze of Rafael. She'd act like an angel during the bimonthly visits from Dona Diana, who'd throw open cupboards, wardrobes, the fridge, inspect under tables, beds, upholstery, quiz the porter, other maids, neighbours, *They tell me...* she'd say hesitantly, *Goodness me, senhora! Surely you're not going to listen to what those people say?*

And then one January, amidst the white and green of the Imperatriz Leopoldinense samba school in Ramos, she met Fafá, cocksure mulatto, chatty, brash, funny, gallant. They became entangled, and the week proved too short for so much loving. They went wild at Carnival – and Sandra awoke on Ash Wednesday to 40 degrees, a desert for a mouth, her head inside out, unable to remember how she'd got back to the apartment, confetti in her henna-straightened hair, glitter shining on her soft black skin, shorts, blouse, high-heeled sandals, worried that a love that had barely begun, might not last Lent. When the sickness started, she nevertheless tried, on streets and corners, in taverns and bars, at drink stalls and huts, *You know Fafá, right? You remember Fafá, right?* fruitlessly.

Protruding belly, one hand in front, one hand behind, she retired to her mother's house, the waters of the Rio Pomba soothing her worries.

Kauê bawled his eyes out, terrifying the new young mother – grandmother took him in her arms, stuck a dummy in his mouth, rocked him, went back to her wittering, my God, what a situation! How are we going to look after this misbegotten child? You stupid girl, you dozy, irresponsible thing! How could you fall for the cheap talk of the first one to come along!? What will become of this little creature? Starting out in life like this, no father, no place to live, he hasn't even got a cot, the poor thing! If it weren't for Maura, if it weren't for Zezé, if it weren't for poor Junim, a single mother! Topic of neighbourhood gossip, ridiculed throughout town, oh, I should never have let her leave home! If only I'd been more firm, but she was stubborn, she'd have torn the house down, I'm going and no one can stop me! And this is the result, shame, dishonour, humiliation... and this bundle of tears for company,

first tooth
first steps
first words
first fall
first naughtiness
first scolding
first communion
first drawing
first schoolbook
first funeral, grandmother's, when not yet eight

until Sandra resolved to go back to Rio de Janeiro, where she'd always belonged – let that dullard Maura look after her godson.

At first Sandra did odd jobs, earning just enough not to have to beg on the streets, until someone from the Zona Sul discovered her, at the checkout of a little supermarket on Avenida Nossa Senhora de Copacabana, and lured her with talk of easy money, lots of it. She was employed as a dancer in a chic Ipanema nightclub and got to know every breed of gringo, German and Japanese, Italian and Portuguese,

Argentinian and French, American and English, well-heeled drooling men who showed their appreciation in dollars. Ladylike, and with a sense of vengeance, she rented a studio flat on Rua São Clemente, Botafogo, with a view of Christ the Redeemer, to banish memories of having lived there in servitude (Marcela and Samuel, now doctors in Cataguases, Rafael, overseas…).

Until her gaze met Fred's shimmering eyes, so fragile, so vacant, a Paulista washed up at a Posto 6 coconut stand. Captivated, she offered to buy him a beer, which his pride reluctantly allowed him to accept. Intrigued, she learned he was an artist, who preferred living in poverty to prostituting himself playing in pretentious bars, *But you'll hear a lot about me one day, just wait and see.* So she fell for him. She took him back to her apartment, gave him a huge gold chain – which he was too ashamed to wear – an imported Ovation guitar, a stereo, music, sunglasses, Lee jeans, All Star trainers, spoiled him, basically, all so she could purr whimsically in his ear.

Sulky, he protested at first, *Just let me record my album, you'll see, I'll get you out of this life, I promise*, then idled away his days, empty beer bottles scattered about the polished floor, ashtrays overflowing with cigarette butts and spliff ends, psychedelic music pouring down the staircase. Bit by bit, he made himself at home: he had friends round, began to disappear without warning, returned dishevelled in the company of strangers, increasingly demanding, imposing, scornful in the way he spoke, dressed, behaved. *Holy shit, Sandra! Get a grip will you!* The money she'd saved was barely enough to sustain them and she stopped sending aid to her sister for Kauê. *I earned nothing this month, Maura, but God willing…* everything staked on one day seeing her man's name, Fred Durão, in every shop window in Rio de Janeiro – the imbeciles in Cataguases will die of envy!

Then she found out she was pregnant. She rehearsed breaking the news to Fred for weeks, afraid of how he'd react, ever more absorbed as he was in dubious company. But when she finally told him, though there was no show of satisfaction, he didn't object to her intention not to abort, *We'll find a way*, he said, distractedly. Head in the clouds, she pictured herself scouring the city shopping centres in search of a special outfit for the infant girl (or will it be a boy?) *This time things will be different...* And she energetically set about fattening a savings account, which she'd opened with Fred, to cover for hard times. Three happy months passed in this flurry of activity, until she awoke one morning to find the studio flat emptied of its electrical appliances, of all clothes, of what little gold they had, of the plentiful jewellery – the savings account plundered. She thought of informing the police, but she was resigned to it, and instead went home to Maura, in Cataguases, as broke as ever.

Later, when she found out she had AIDs – her and Kaíke, still at the breast – she turned to Doctor Samuel, who appealed to Social Security and managed to get her a basic benefit allowance she collected from the Caixa the first Thursday of every month. And she was the talk of the town in Ana Carrara, that Sandra's a lucky one, instead of living like a woodlouse in Cataguases, loading and unloading a washing machine or buried inside a textile mill, she'd seen the world, got smart, wise, cunning, and now she gets to parade around the city streets like a peacock...

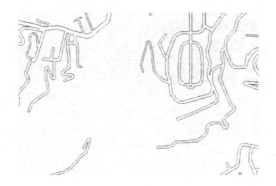

Strangers

Sérgio Sant'Anna

Translated by Julia Sanches

I ARRIVED AT the entrance to the building in Botafogo where I'd be visiting a flat at almost the same time she did. I noticed how nervous she was in the way she took small successive drags of her cigarette, in the way she gripped the newspaper's classifieds, and also the way her lipstick spilled over her lips, as if hastily applied. This didn't make her any less beautiful or elegant in her burlap dress, which boasted of a simplicity that must have cost a pretty penny. Her large black shoes were the kind that lace up, giving her a slightly exotic look, an air of strength, almost of brutality – perhaps premeditated – a slightly masculine touch that did not in any way overwhelm the feminine in her. Or maybe this only came to me afterwards, after I was finally able to write about her in this way. Right then, I was worried about seeing the flat.

When the doorman handed me the keys, because I had arrived first, she said, with the same affected toughness as her shoes:

'Can't we all go up together?'

The doorman took the keys back and dangled them from his fingers as if we were children fighting over sweets.

'I'm very sorry, ma'am, but I can't leave the lobby,' he said. 'The flat's empty and, if you don't mind, you could go see it with the gentleman here.' The doorman pointed at me with the keys.

She looked me up and down, as if sizing me up, and concluded I was inoffensive.

57

'Fine by me,' she said.

That meticulous examination, or perhaps its result, irritated me. As did the fact that the doorman had asked her if *she* didn't mind going up with *me*, instead of asking me, who had arrived before her, if I minded going up with her. At the end of the day, we were fighting over the same flat. I shrugged, indifferent.

As soon as I had, she grabbed the keys from the doorman and walked down the alleyway, or whatever you call that open-air passageway that borders the parking lot, and which led to Block B, where the flat was located.

As I walked after her, I thought of how I had no real desire to live in that condominium, composed of two vertical blocks, and which had the ridiculous name Bois de Boulogne. There was in fact a garden, as well as some trees, which aimed to make the space seem bucolic and green. There was also a playground, which would mean lots of children when they weren't in school, and, hidden somewhere, a pool (I'd read in the classifieds), which was probably actually a large water tank, which would also be teeming with children. To be honest, what Clarice and I really wanted was to begin our new life together in one of those old buildings with a more human architecture, and we had no intention whatsoever of having children so early on. But I was going to see the flat. I was on holiday and scheduled to go flat hunting.

After walking up two small flights of stairs, I reached the woman, standing in the hall between the Block B lifts, and we behaved as the strangers we were to each other. She placed a cigarette between her lips, leaving it unlit. Another woman joined us. The lift arrived soon after, a few people got out, we let the woman walk in before us, then she walked in, and finally I did the same. The other woman got off on the fifth floor. She had spent the whole journey staring grumpily at the unlit cigarette between the lips of the woman, who steadily held her gaze. As soon as the woman got out, she lit her cigarette, despite the No Smoking sign visible through

58

the childish graffiti, some Nazi-themed, others just obscene. As an ex-smoker, I wasn't one to be bothered by her cigarette.

'Have you been flat hunting long?' I asked to break the ice between us.

'No. This is the second. They're all shit.'

'It's true,' I said to appease her, finding it funny.

We arrived on the eleventh floor, *our* flat's floor, and I noticed her hand trembling as she tried to unlock the door. I excused myself, took the key from her and easily inserted it in the keyhole.

She walked in and looked around until she found the bathroom, in which she immediately locked herself. Despite being autumn, it was hot and stuffy, and I went to open the living room window. The first thing I noticed, as I looked out at the view, were people walking up and down the anthill-like *favela* – it's impossible to be original in these matters – less than a kilometre away. I looked down, spotting the pool. It was a slight improvement on a water tank, and since there was no one in it, was probably closed at that time of the afternoon. The playground, on the other hand, was starting to fill up, their yells reaching the apartment, and yet there were fewer children than I'd originally imagined. I took note of a few more bits and bobs around the building, trying also to see the surroundings through Clarice's eyes.

I noticed that the woman was taking her time in the toilet and became suddenly suspicious. Surely not Cocaine? And anyway, I wasn't *with* her. I could just take a look around the flat on my own and leave, since I'd already more or less decided that the building wasn't to Clarice's taste.

As I turned to better examine the living room, I noticed a few irregularities on the wall in front of me, which the sun was just then striking. The mortar and the paint had been recently retouched in certain places, forming small lumps. As I approached the wall, so I could inspect them closely, the woman exited the bathroom. She was smoking again and had reapplied her lipstick. She had also made up her eyes, which shone, red. It could've been cocaine since her nose seemed congested, but it also occurred to me that she could simply have been crying, and that she had wanted to cover it up with make-up.

I pretended not to notice and prodded one of the lumps, which gave way slightly.

'They could be bullet holes,' I said. 'They must have taken the bullets out, which is why the rent is so cheap.'

I noticed I was trying to impress her, which, to judge by her response, I didn't succeed in doing.

'You think it's cheap, for a pigsty like this? You've got to see the toilet. It's ridiculous!'

'I mean, in terms of market value.'

'Maybe,' she said, looking towards the window, 'but the *favela* is quite far.'

'Bullets can travel up to two kilometres,' I said, noticing I was still trying to impress her.

'Are you a cop?' she asked with a fake neutrality and ingenuity to her voice, which was obviously sarcastic.

'No, I'm a journalist.'

She walked toward the window without asking which newspaper I worked for or the kind of journalism I practised, and I thought it best that way. Because, and I don't really know why, I thought I'd feel like an idiot if I told a woman like her that I was the subeditor for the society pages, conducting phone interviews and writing nonsense about narcissistic artists.

She chucked her fag end out the window and watched it fall. Then she turned to me and said, before leaning once again on the windowsill:

'It's a good height.'

The thought suddenly came to me that she had only come to see the flat to throw herself from it. I might have just been projecting, of course. I'm also somewhat neurotic and had been in therapy before I met Clarice, who gave me a sense of security. But I decided, just in case, to walk back to the window, from where I could intervene if the woman ever hinted at the possibility of jumping. I must confess that, beside the fact that I didn't want a fellow human being to self-destruct, I was also thinking of all the possible complications, with the police, the press, and with Clarice. How exactly would I explain to her that I had visited a flat with another woman who, on top of it all, had thrown herself from it?

But, as soon as I reached the woman, she said:

'I'm going to take a look around.'

While she went to check out one of the rooms facing the back of the building, I looked at another one, right opposite hers, trying to shake the thought of suicide from my head. To be honest, I knew I'd left therapy before I'd had the chance to unsettle certain deeper murky waters, and perhaps precisely so I wouldn't have to. And yet this woman, despite it all, struck me as someone who truly liked life. It just had to be the life she liked.

The room I entered was standard, one of those small, square-shaped ones builders use to get the most out of a space. It had also recently been painted, but I could see no lumps on the walls. I opened the window and then decided to take a quick look at the fitted wardrobe. I tried to open one of the drawers and realised something was making it jam. I pulled it open with force and a dusty bra came loose. I held it and observed that, due to its size and design, a woman with small breasts, probably on the younger side, must have worn it.

Just then I heard her say something in the other room that I failed to hear clearly, though, from where I stood, I could see her holding an object I couldn't quite make out. I quickly put the bra back in the drawer and immediately closed it.

'Come see!' the woman said, loudly.

I walked quickly towards her and found her holding a

strip of bamboo blind, which she was unrolling on the floor, where it must have been left during the move. There was a fair-sized hole in it.

'Bullets!' the woman said, with a kind of joy, even though there was only one hole. 'The bullet must have entered through the other room, crossed the hallway and ended up here. Actually, it may even have gone out again,' she signalled towards the open window. 'You were right. Those good-for-nothings left this crap here' – she dropped the curtain with disgust – 'thinking we wouldn't notice.'

Satisfied by her recognition, I added, excitedly:

'I saw only a handful of children in the playground. There must be loads of people leaving the building.'

And that was when she said the phrase that allowed me to finally understand her better.

'Dying doesn't matter. What's awful is growing old!'

'You're far from that,' I said, feeling half-idiot half-scumbag. But I saw a spark in her eyes.

'I'm thirty-four,' the woman said, and she looked at me expectantly.

'You look a lot younger,' I said, even though she could also have been 36. 'And even though you don't look it, it's a good age.'

'He doesn't seem to think so,' she retorted, bitterly.

'He, who?'

'Doesn't matter. And you, how old are you?'

'Thirty-two.'

'He's fifty,' she said proudly.

And that's when I said something really stupid, but then again maybe not, if you take into account what happened afterwards:

'Did he leave you?'

Without any warning, she broke into convulsive tears of pain and rage and walked towards me with clenched fists. I retreated, startled. But, instead of hitting me, she clung to my body and rubbed hers on mine in a fervent rhythmic motion.

I looked towards the window, worried someone could see us, but luckily there were no tall buildings around.

'No one has ever left me, you understand?' she yelled. 'You hear me? No one!'

'Of course,' I said, hugging her back mechanically, still frightened.

'The son of a bitch is fucking someone else,' she said, finally crying freely.

I touched her hair paternally:

'Is that why you're looking for a flat?'

She nodded yes: 'He's fucking an eighteen-year-old girl. Do you know what that means?'

'I do,' I said. And in fact I did understand it all more and more. 'These things happen,' I tried consoling her.

Which made her push me, viciously.

'You're all the same. Don't think I didn't see you holding that bra. *I* don't even need to wear one, see!'

She pulled her dress up, all at once. She'd stopped crying just as suddenly as she'd started.

She had perfect breasts. So, maybe she'd had some plastic surgery done, but what did it matter if they were so beautiful, so *hot*? All I could do then was touch them, as I slid my hand in her white knickers and she undid my belt, lowering my trousers and my boxers in one go and kneeling at my feet to suck my cock, making it grow immensely, which seemed to intensely satisfy her and which may not have actually had anything to do with me – I could see in her snake eyes – but with the guy who was fucking the eighteen-year-old, as if she wanted to prove how powerful she was to him and which she ended up proving to me, and well.

I asked for a break, since otherwise it would come to an end too soon, and also so I could take off my shirt and my shoes, around which my trousers and my pants had become tangled, and making it so that I had to lean on her head not to lose my balance.

While I took everything off, she removed her knickers:
'Shoes on or off?' she asked.

'On,' I said.

She let out a short laugh:

'I knew it. You're all just closet homosexuals.'

I ignored her comment, since I'm not sexist, and instead decided to meticulously observe her ostensive and yet well-proportioned cunt, which was pleasing to look at, with its little, trimmed bush.

She seemed to take pleasure in how I looked at her and calmly lit a cigarette.

'You really smoke, don't you?' I said, just because. Or maybe it was because that contemplative silence had left me feeling a little embarrassed.

In response, she took a long, provocative drag from her fag, walked towards me and asked me to kiss her on the mouth. It was one of those deep, sexual kisses that have very little to do with the kisses of people in love. As we kissed, she slowly blew smoke into my mouth. I'd only quit smoking because of Clarice, who was militantly anti-tobacco; I didn't cough nor choke, on the contrary: I sucked the smoke in deeply, keeping it in my lungs as long as I could. If words alone could describe that experience, I'd have to say she drove me as crazy as if I were an opium-smoker, and that it was the most intimate experience I have ever had with a woman, as if I knew the deepest parts of her. Being out of practice, though, it just made me feel vaguely dizzy and so I lowered my body, taking hers with me.

'Do you want me to do something with you that I always do with him?' she asked.

'Yes,' I said, still feeling unsteady.

'Turn around then.'

I snapped out of my stupor and raised my head, scared:

'Only if you put out that cigarette.'

'I'm not into S&M,' she said disdainfully, putting out her fag on the parquet.

I turned around and she came up over me, in a way that allowed me to better understand the way women work, or at least certain women, and also men, or at least certain men, men like me and like that depraved old letch. Rhythmically rubbing her cunt on my arse, she would say things like, 'Honey, I adore you, I'm going to eat you right up.' And that's how she came, of which there was no doubt, since there was nothing theatrical in her orgasm. It was just a series of silent tremors and little, almost introspective pants, after which she fell beside me, satisfied. Then she laid her head on my chest and started drawing lines on it with her pointed nails.

'Please don't do that,' I said.

'Why not?' she continued, with even more force.

I held her arms:

'I'm engaged.'

She let out a fake cackle and got up abruptly:

'I can't believe it. It's almost the twenty-first century and you're engaged? Where's your ring?'

'I don't wear one. There's nothing formal. Clarice and I are going to get married.'

'Alright, in that case maybe you should leave,' she said, turning to where she'd thrown her things. 'I don't want to get mixed up in your life. How old is Clarice?' she asked, trying to sound casual.

'Nineteen,' I said, even though Clarice was 24. The only reason I didn't say eighteen is because it would seem like too much of a coincidence.

If there had been something in the room to throw against the wall, I'm sure she would have thrown it. But as there wasn't, she just kicked the air, trying to kick her shoes off, which she didn't manage, since they were firmly strapped to her. She put on her dress, though inside out. As she took it off again, she almost strangled herself with it, unlike the first time, when she had been graceful and sure. And so she ended up naked again, her shoes on, quietly crying, as if it had all somehow aged her suddenly and made her accept the reality of things.

I'm not stupid, despite the fact that the things I've written for the society pages often were. I remained lying down, naked, waiting for her hysteria to pass. I knew that if she didn't commit an act from which there was no return, the fact that I had a nineteen-year-old girlfriend would make her desire grow, this time for me, even if only to prove something. And, wiping away her tears, she ended up asking the inevitable million-dollar question.

'Did you bring a condom?'

'No, Clarice and I are monogamous. We don't use them.'

'But he and I aren't and we don't trust anyone,' she said, going to the spot where she'd dropped her bag. She rummaged around in it and then threw me a condom.

'I was going to use it with that cunt,' she made a point of telling me. 'But if you do anything perverted with me, I'll scream.'

'What would be perverted?'

'If you get anywhere near it, I'll let you know,' she said.

I went to put the thing on in the toilet, where I was dying to take a piss. There, I tried to figure out what she had found so ridiculous about it, since it seemed to be fairly standard, even comfortable, with images of blue Venuses and angels playing trumpets, probably copied secondhand from a toilet in some European palace. And I couldn't stop thinking, annoyingly, how Clarice would have liked that toilet, how she would have thought it was the best part of the apartment.

Or had the woman meant the oval mirror, with its intricate silver frame? The mirror I was now looking at myself in, observing how my face had somehow changed, perhaps because of a certain loss of innocence, given that I was betraying Clarice for the first time. I tried searching within myself for some old familiar sense of guilt, but couldn't find it. I concluded that it had not been a betrayal, but was simply an occurrence as inexorable as a catastrophe. I had been knocked down by destiny and now all I could do was meet it headfirst.

I found the woman in the living room, lying on her back on a small mattress she said she'd found in the maid's room. She was naked all the way to her shoes and, with her eyes and legs half-open, she looked like the bride she was certainly playing, with a slight rosiness to her cheeks, which may have been rouge, but what did it matter?

Descriptions of the minutiae of sex are inelegant and dull. If I have commented on them previously, it is because I found particular acts to have obeyed a certain radical logic and motivation, a rare – and why not say refined? – kind of sexuality that might someday enrich the reader of this story, written by one who does not claim to be anything more than a reporter.

But I believe that what I *can* say is that we used two condoms and that we did everything in that second run except for what, I imagined, she would have considered a perversion. As for her orgasms in the second phase, they were almost certainly fake and theatrical and, at times, I was forced to cover her mouth. But what does it matter, since mine were real, as real as my emotions?

Perhaps my greatest mistake was to attempt to translate these emotions, commenting on the setting sun, on the moonlight bathing our bodies, or on the autumnal cicadas' evening song. And at one point I even said, with a certain tenderness:

'We could even die together.'

This reminded her she had to leave.

'It'd be better if we left separately, after the fuss we kicked up. I'll go first and then you can hand in the keys, OK?' she said.

'Are you going to take the flat?' I asked, as we dressed.

'This prison cell? You've got to be kidding me.'

'Are you going to go back to that guy?'

'Now I can,' she said.

'Are you going to tell him what happened?' I asked, kneeling to tie my laces as she lit another cigarette.

'Anything's possible,' she said. 'But I don't recommend you do the same. Your little girlfriend wouldn't forgive you.'

'Maybe I don't want to be forgiven.'

'You're crazy,' she said, walking towards the door.

I wanted to walk her to the lift, but she wouldn't let me.

'At least tell me your name,' I begged.

'What happened happened, right? What do names matter?'

'You don't want to know mine?'

'No,' she said as she slammed the door.

What else is there to say?

I broke up with Clarice, started smoking again and came here to live on my own, paying pennies for the rent in apartment 1101 B, in the Bois de Boulogne condominium, with the hope – and perhaps under the fantastical notion, at least as concerns the second half of my hope – that that old fart would mess around with another bird and that the woman would somehow sniff me out for some more revenge.

Up until this moment, as I write this, it hasn't happened. But, despite long intervals of more or less tedious calm, there is a lot going on in the *Bois* and its roundabouts: clashes between traffickers on Dona Marta, the popping of rifles and machine guns, flares piercing the air, police and military raids in the *favela*, helicopters flying nap-of-the-earth over the neighbourhood and, now and then, stray bullets that have once again perforated the bedroom and living room walls.

Sometimes, I crawl through the dark and go lie on the wooden floor of the room where that woman possessed me. Entrenched behind a wall, I light a cigarette, take a deep drag and think of her who penetrated me to the core.

I switched the society pages for the police section, bought a pair of powerful binoculars so that I could watch the hill, and set up a fax machine in the empty room where the maid would normally live and whose mattress, on which I sometimes sleep, I have kept. From there, the second safest place in the building, I send the latest news to the editorial room, at times just minutes before *Cidade*'s press deadline. I write it by hand, and that's exactly how I send off the pages, since my dictaphone took a bullet, wiping its memory forever, in the same way a human being is wiped out. We're ahead of all our competitors when it comes to news about Dona Marta.

One Sunday, while I stared absently out the window, I witnessed how a man wearing a pair of longish swimming trunks was struck by a sniper as he dove into the condominium's semi-deserted pool. He was probably dead when he hit the water, its blue tinged red, a macabre blend on that sunny spring day. That was exactly how I wrote it and they didn't change a word.

I thought also of how perhaps dying didn't matter in the least. The man had exited the stage with great style, while we, here, continue suffering for various reasons, including my own.

And I wasn't just tossing off a line when I wrote at the end of that piece, and in the hope that the woman might read it, finally understand and come in search of me: *dying is easy in the Bois de Boulogne.*

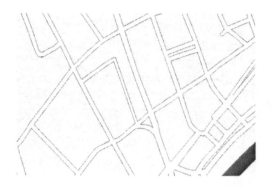

Decembers

Marcelo Moutinho

Translated by Kim M. Hastings

I

I'M TEN AND I love my grandpa.

He's the one who brings me to school, because Dad works and Mum has to take care of Emilia. We leave our house on Travessa do Liceu at six thirty and go along Rua Sacadura Cabral, where there's a really good snack bar. I get a ham and cheese roll and sugarcane juice. My grandpa has bread and butter and black coffee in a short glass. Always in a glass. If the waiter serves the coffee in a cup, he complains. Complains without saying anything, just shaking his head. Because Grandpa doesn't talk. I'll get to that later.

The roll with juice is my favourite part of the walk. Second is looking at the cars in the parking lot right before the street my school is on. All those cars, each one nicer than the next. But Grandpa doesn't like them. He scowls. Dad said it's because in Grandpa's time cars were much better made, they didn't dent so easily. Sometimes at home Grandpa shows me a photo of an old blue car. It was called 'Willys Aero'. Dad said it was a fancy car.

Now I'm going to explain why Grandpa doesn't talk. Mum said that he used to talk and all of a sudden stopped. I never heard it, must have been before I was born. But he's not dumb. He sings, he just doesn't talk. But his voice is there.

I already know some of the songs by heart – they're

73

always the same old ones. My mum told me that they're songs from Rádio Nacional. They were big hits, everyone knew them. And Rádio Nacional was right next door to our house. I think my grandpa was a singer.

One day I asked Grandpa to take me into the building where the radio station was, but he wouldn't.

And I don't care that Grandpa doesn't talk. He taught me how to kick the ball into the goal, how to make paper aeroplanes that really fly, and not to touch a socket without wearing rubber-soled shoes. Some days he doesn't want to play and spends the afternoon listening to old records. I stay in his room with him. He sings and I draw with coloured pencils. Afterwards, I show him the drawings. Only him.

On my birthday, Grandpa takes me to the McDonald's on Avenida Rio Branco. That makes me happy. Since my birthday is the week of Christmas, the trees are all decorated with lights, and the street is full of people passing by. At the very end of the year, we go all the way down Rio Branco to Cinelândia to watch the confetti falling from the buildings like snow.

We like to watch TV too. You know those game shows people compete on? Well, we like those. I root for one contestant and my grandpa roots for another. That's the game we play. He gets mad when his contestant loses.

Come to think of it, I spend more time with Grandpa than I do with Mum and Dad. And we never argue. I don't know if that's because he doesn't talk, but we never argue. So I think Grandpa's great.

II

I'm seventeen and I hate my grandfather.

Rereading the composition I wrote when I was little, I can't believe how stupid I was. Back then I was a student at the Vicente Licínio Cardoso School, which still exists today. Tia Tânia was my teacher. She marked my mistakes in red, reworked sentences, moved everything around. If I'd written it like that, I would have gotten a 10, not a 7. Tia Tânia assigned the class to write a composition about our grandfathers. Whoever didn't have one could choose an older uncle or someone who was like a grandfather.

I had a grandfather and thought he was great. I can't understand why, because he's a walking embarrassment. He only speaks by singing, no one takes him seriously. People make fun of him in public. I'm ashamed to leave the house with him.

My grandfather has all kinds of weird habits. He listens to records instead of just downloading music. And only oldies. The singers sound like they're going to die from so much suffering, and they wail. My grandfather wails along, he must think that he's still a singer and that his room is the Rádio Nacional.

When I switched schools, I asked him to stop going with me in the morning. He kept it up for a week or two. As soon as we got to the entrance, everyone gave me a hard time because I was old enough to be coming on my own. The worst is that my grandfather doesn't know how to match his clothes. He wears shorts with shoes and socks. And tucks dress shirts into his shorts. Ridiculous.

So he started taking Emilia to school, the same one I went to.

My grandfather doesn't get that I'm not a kid anymore. I don't feel like kicking the ball against the wall and I'm sick of hearing that if you stick your finger in a socket without having rubber-soled shoes on, blah blah blah.

When I go out, he really tests my patience. One night, he came looking for me at the Kalesa Cabaret. I wasn't even going in since you have to be eighteen. My friends and I planned to just hang out by the door, watching the freaks who go there. Then my grandfather showed up and tried to take me home. No one let me forget that. To this day they call me grandpa's little boy.

Sometimes I feel sorry for him and agree to do something. Go to the McDonald's on Rio Branco, for instance. But I confess that it's boring. He doesn't say anything, I have nothing to say to him, and the two of us sit there in silence, sipping our shakes and chewing our burgers.

If I want to go fishing with the guys off the Perimetral, I have to do it secretly. Because if my grandfather even suspects, he'll blab to my dad, who will call and tell me that the overpass is dangerous, that I could fall from up there, and that fish from polluted water are no good.

Just like the nightclubs in the neighbourhood are no good. Be careful, those places are full of trouble, Dad says. When your granddad was young, it wasn't like that. It's all gone downhill.

Dad said that we ended up living there because of my grandfather's job. Since he got out of the radio station late, he needed to live nearby. After years of paying rent, when prices dropped around here, he bought our apartment through the Credit Union. Thirty years of paying, Dad reminds me every time this subject comes up.

This area was really different, teeming with artists. Orlando Silva, Francisco Alves, Marlene, Linda Batista. We named your sister after Emilinha, one of your grandfather's favourites, Dad said.

I don't know those singers. Nor do any of my friends. I just know they don't live here. I think my grandfather is the only one left.

III

I'm 25 and I no longer have a grandfather.

Now the room he lived in is mine. I sold his old records at the Praça Quinze flea market, replaced the furniture, and changed the wall colour. I planned to redo the floor too but ran out of money. The only things remaining were my drawings. The ones I did with coloured pencils while my grandfather sang, which he kept.

That was one of the discoveries about my grandfather. There were others when I watched the mini-series *Dalva and Herivelto* that aired on Globo TV. Dalva de Oliveira and Herivelto Martins were Rádio Nacional success stories, like those artists my dad talks about.

Watching the mini-series, I recognised some of the songs my grandfather used to sing.

Let's Walk Away, which I called 'No, I can't remember that I loved you'. The Ave Maria song that always reminds me of the São Bento Monastery. That other one about the fish deep in the net; I thought that was a funny image. And *Grey Hairs*, which he would sing pointing to his own head. I always laughed when he did that.

The mini-series made me want to know which programme my grandfather was involved with during the days of Rádio Nacional. For the first time, I went into the building where the station was. It backs up against our house. Almost all the floors are taken up today by an organisation called the National Institute of Industrial Property. The radio station still exists and continues there but is limited to a few floors. I found out from the receptionist that the building was designed by a Frenchman, constructed in 1929, is art deco in style, and serves as an architectural landmark. Nothing about my grandfather.

It became an obsession. I started leaving the bank at four every afternoon and holing up in the National Library to read publications on the 1940s and 50s. I pored through books, newspapers, issues of the *Revista do Rádio*. Not one mention of my grandfather's name.

My mother and father refused to shed any further light. They simply said that yes, he worked at the Rádio Nacional, and that's why we lived on Travessa do Liceu.

The few personal papers he left behind didn't help either. A dance card from the Eldorado. Old forms of ID.

Pension pay stubs. No reference to the radio station.

Almost all the neighbours knew that my grandfather had worked there but not exactly what he did. Your granddad was always discreet, they would say, and then he got quiet, self-contained.

I'd almost given up when I finally managed, with my year-end bonus, to pull together the money to install the porcelain floor in my room. It was a Saturday afternoon, the last week of December. I was clearing lunch from the table when the tiler, who was removing the wooden flooring, called me over. Beneath one of the boards was a paper wrapped in plastic. He handed it to me.

I went back to the kitchen and removed the plastic.

EMPLOYEE NO. 576
—*Domingos Santana da Silva*—
Kitchen staff

It was my grandfather's Rádio Nacional badge.

I tucked the badge back into the plastic. Since work was being done in the bedroom, I stowed it in a drawer of the hall cupboard.

I'm going out, I informed the tiler. I'll be back soon. And I set out for McDonald's.

I went down the steps, the back of the radio building to my left, and imagined my grandfather cheerfully pouring coffee for the artists, grilling a ham and cheese sandwich to perfection. My grandfather, who was a singer and worked at the Rádio Nacional.

I crossed Rua do Acre, went into McDonald's, and ordered a milkshake. Keep the change.

At the corner, I turned right. Rio Branco was one long, light-coloured carpet.

Cup in hand, I began to stroll toward Cinelândia, feeling the confetti falling from the buildings brush my shoulders before reaching the ground.

The Woman Who Slept with a Horse

João Ximenes Braga

Translated by Zoë Perry

THE WOMAN WHO was run over and wanted to make sure she got her settlement. The young man looking for career success. The lady trying to assure herself her husband was faithful. Standing in the queue, Andréa had no choice but to listen to the stories, without any sympathy for the people telling them. She felt only weariness at the abundance of details.

Their stories were no more pathetic than Andréa's, which is why she disdained them so much. Each new story only heightened her own discomfort about being in that queue, and the fear of not having the courage to speak when it was her turn.

The suggestion had come from a friend who was even more of a sceptic than she was. 'It can't hurt. It makes more sense than feng shui.' Her friend's life had noticeably improved when he started going regularly to the Umbanda *terreiro*. He never fully admitted the direct connection between the two. It might be just a coincidence, chance; either way, he wasn't going to dismiss its merits. As he reiterated to Andréa: 'It can't hurt.'

The friend in question was one of the few to whom Andréa revealed the entirety of her clichéd existence: successful career woman at 27 (though there was never anything left of her paycheque from the publishers she worked at, come the end of each month, thanks to her instalment plans at various imported clothing boutiques), but profoundly lonely.

She was beautiful, but quite unlike the conventional type men found alluring. Her harsh and angular features, the face of a 1920s Hollywood vamp, rarely intrigued her contemporaries, more interested in a type of beauty that whispers submission.

Andréa occupied a particular category in a world of categorised relationships. She didn't pay much attention to this, just lamented belonging to the category that came out losing. And she had already grown weary of being with the sort of man who left her apartment before she awoke, or who left after eating all her Minas cheese, never to be heard from again. She wanted to break the cycle and meet a guy who might very well eat all her cheese, but would then go down to the bakery to buy fresh bread and return, eager to stay the afternoon. For that, for so little, she was there in that queue, waiting to be seen by the Exu Tranca-Rua, who her friend had recommended, listening to that parade of whinging from people devoid of self-irony, who considered their problems to be of great consequence. Andréa thought she was above them, because at least she felt ridiculous for being there. As if that guaranteed the integrity of her intelligence.

And there she was, confident of her ridiculousness, seated on the reinforced concrete floor around the small dirt yard where the spirits conducted their work, listening to the drumbeats coming from inside the house where the proper spiritual centre operated, when Mr T.R., as her friend playfully referred to his guide, Exu Tranca-Rua, addressed her.

'Dontcha have any enemies, child?'

'Pardon?'

The short woman beside her, in a lime green leotard that highlighted her outspread belly over a pair of avocado green leggings, explained things to Andréa.

'He's going to burn the enemies now. Write down the name of your enemy and give it to him.'

'But I don't have any enemies.'

She hesitated.

'Not that I know of.'

'Then you can write "unknown enemy",' suggested the lady in green on green, handing her a strip of paper and a pen.

'Well, Miss? I'm waiting,' Mr T.R. said insistently.

Andréa hurriedly wrote down 'unknown enemy' and stepped onto the dirt-floored area to hand the paper to the Exu. For a second she even wondered, if she did, in fact, have an actual enemy, whether she might be sending somebody to their death, or an accident, or something like that, and nearly chickened out. But that thought didn't last long. As soon as the soles of her bare feet felt the ground, still damp from the afternoon rain, she was comforted by memories of her childhood on the farm, and felt at home for the first time since she'd arrived there. She quickly remembered her displeased father when she had decided to move to the big city on her own to study. Her father was afraid she would become a stray. Which, technically, taking into consideration his paternal ideas and her own, as different as they were, she, in fact, was.

When she handed the paper to Mr T.R., she was finally able to observe him up close. The first time she saw him, when she arrived at the *terreiro* a few hours earlier and asked a girl in white for her name be included in the queue for visits with Exu Tranca-Rua, all she could do was laugh. The black velvet cape with an embroidered trident on the back in red sequins. The black top hat with a chicken feather stuck in the brim. The white trousers that looked like pyjama bottoms. It was all so ridiculous. The only reason she didn't walk right back out the door was because her friend had prepared her for this. 'Yeah, he looks a bit like someone out of a campy horror film, like Coffin Joe. He's a little theatrical, or cinematic, in the Ed Wood sense of the word. But remember it's all a ritual. If you think about it, it's no more carnivalesque than what a Catholic bishop wears, or a Tibetan monk.'

Now, however, seeing him up close, she could see the man under the props. His strong face framed by a thick, greying beard, his muscular bare chest, also covered in thick, greying hair, contrasting with his copper-coloured skin. 'He's interesting,' thought Andréa, with a shudder. 'He must have a big dick.' She liked excesses.

Tranca-Rua added her paper to the others in the clay bowl, and Andréa realised it was time for her to return to the concrete. He covered the papers with a black powder, and warned everyone:

'This is gunpowder, be careful.'

The lit match fell on the bowl and up rose black smoke. Andréa noticed that everyone around her was wiping their hands over their bodies, like they were dusting off their clothes. She duplicated the gesture. As she did so, she remembered a few people who really could be considered her enemies, and felt as if from that moment they could no longer reach her. And she felt comforted by the sight of the Exu behind the smoke, magnified by the burning embers' hypnotic dance, a special effect that warranted him a cinematic, if not divine, quality. She went from being bored to anxious, itching for her turn to approach the spirit.

Until her turn arrived.

'What do you want, my child?' asked the Exu with his deep voice, quickly, in an ambiguous accent.

'Um, I don't know.'

Andréa didn't realise it, but she was acting just the way she would if she were being chatted up: she was playing hard to get. Not in the sense of consciously hindering the process, to follow the basic rules of the cliché. Andréa played hard to get naturally, because she had never matured enough to go beyond the logic of a prepubertal child, in which attraction to the opposite sex is translated into pure aggression. And that was how, without realising, she was acting with Exu Tranca-Rua.

'So what are you doing here?'

'Uh, a friend told me to come.'

He bit down hard on his cigar, took a long puff, and then Andréa became a bit frightened: she had clearly exhausted his patience. Even without knowing much about Umbanda, she knew that couldn't be good.

'I'm gonna do something, Miss, to see if you can't clear your mind.'

He took the cigar and puffed smoke along Andréa's torso. She couldn't contain her laughter. He turned to her. Their eyes met. And Andréa realised her spontaneous giggling fit had been very, very misinterpreted by the spirit. She got goose bumps for the second time, but this time they weren't because she was horny.

'I'm sorry, Tranca-Rua. It's just that I'm new at this. I've never been to a *terreiro* before.'

'And why'd you come now?'

'Well, I'm a little lost, you know? Things at work are pretty good, but my love life…'

Mr T.R. made it clear he had no patience for dramatic pauses.

'You want a man?'

'No. I mean, not just any man. I just wanted to have the chance to meet someone nice.'

'Write this down, so you don't forget. Seven red candles. Seven black candles. You're gonna take 'em to a crossroads. You can go at night, cos some people are real embarrassed to be *macumbeiro*. Light the candles and make an offering to me and to Maria Mulambo. Leave without turnin' your back on the candles and then don't look back.'

'But if I can't turn my back on them, how am I not going to look back?'

'Child, you leave without your back turned, when you get to the crossroads you can turn around, but then you can't look back anymore.'

'Oh, alright. Well… Thanks, okay?'

'Run along, Miss. I've got more to do.'

Andréa hated fluorescent light. She bowed to the imperious necessity to go to the Mangueira samba school only because it was the inescapable thing to do that December Saturday evening in Rio. She wasn't good at dancing samba, and she felt intimidated even trying. She was bothered by the stifling heat in the place, which made her skin shiny, breathing difficult, and tasted of cheap cigarettes. But above all, she hated the effect of the fluorescent light on her shiny skin.

Her girlfriends, extremely drunk, jumped up and down on the dance floor unceremoniously, even though they were just as bad as her at the intricate ankle movements demanded by the percussion, which she had been ignoring for some time, aided by the terrible acoustics. Andréa offered to get some beers, not so much because she was thirsty, but because she wanted to walk – that is, to move without having to try to follow a rhythm that was alien to her own. As she waded through the wall of sweaty bodies, mixing bodily fluids without the pleasure generally associated with that image, she wondered how long before she could convince her group of friends to leave without risking looking like a party-pooper. She wanted to get out of there, even if it was just to sit on a cold metal chair at some hole in the wall in Buraco Quente. At least there the beer would be cold, there was the chance someone with a career might turn up, and she could sit down.

Of course, as soon as she sat down in Buraco Quente, she would wonder if it wouldn't be better to go to Cervantes, because maybe one of their sausage and pineapple sandwiches would make her feel better. At Cervantes, she would wonder if maybe they should go to the Guanabara pizzeria, to watch actors on the rise to stardom, and actors on the decline, and tawdry blondes in tight trousers with their brawny boyfriends strutting about. It would keep her entertained for a few minutes. At Guanabara, she would wonder if that DJ whose music she'd hated, but whose bed she had used two weeks ago, might be at Jobi having one for the road. At Jobi, she would ask around if there was still something going on at Zero Zero, or if it might be worth stopping by the after-party at Dama de Ferro, where she could meet her gay friends and give up on meeting a guy that night, even though she would still scrutinise the dance floor upon her arrival in search of a straight man.

Andréa wanted to be everywhere, because she never wanted to be anywhere. She especially did not want to be at home. If she actually thought about it, she would realise that she didn't even want to be in her own body. But she wasn't thinking about any of that, at the Mangueira samba school. She just walked through the sweaty bodies, trying to slip between the other people with as little contact as possible, getting even more annoyed when she came up against the smile of someone who appeared to genuinely surrender to the percussion, to the dance, to the alcohol.

Buying the beers was complicated: opening her purse, finding the money, shouting the quantity to the seller, receiving her change in damp one-*Real* notes which, disgusted, she stuck in her purse. Finally she found herself with three cans of cold beer in her hands, which made moving between sweaty bodies toward her cluster of friends all the more difficult. By her first step, she already recognised a face. That is… at first she didn't recognise it, didn't identify it, just realised that she had seen it before, but where? It was the Exu!

Andréa only realised she was smiling gleefully at him when she saw he hadn't recognised her. He smiled naughtily back at her out of the corner of his mouth. It was a flirtatious smile. Andréa felt embarrassed and her own smile faded. He gave a slight nod, as a formal greeting, without changing his expression, and she kept going. She walked through the sweaty bodies carelessly, making no attempt to safeguard the cans of beer or her own body from contact with others. Confused, the sound of the samba percussion returned to her ears, a sound she had mentally blocked out hours earlier.

When she reunited with her group, she handed out two cans of beer, opened one for herself and spotted the friend who had recommended the Umbanda *terreiro* to her.

'You'll never guess who I just saw,' she said, struggling to find that delicate place of balance in her voice, so she could hear herself over the music, but wasn't screaming so loudly that she popped the poor guy's eardrums, or could be heard by the other sweaty bodies brushing against hers.

'What?'

'You'll never guess who I just saw!' she repeated, striking a new tone.

'Who?'

'Mr T.R.'

'Who?'

'Mr T.R., Tranca-Rua.'

'Oh, yeah. He always comes to Mangueira.'

'He didn't even say hello to me properly.'

'What?'

'He pretended like he didn't even fucking know me! You think he was embarrassed to see me outside the *terreiro*?'

'Oh, sometimes the horses don't remember.'

'What?'

'They don't remember. The horses.'

'What horse?'

'The horse, dammit. "Horse" is what they call the medium, the guy who embodies the spirit. They don't always remember what they did afterward, not even the people they talked to.'

'You've got to be kidding me.'

'I'm not kidding. You spoke with a spirit. The spirit left. The guy who's here is just a regular guy who comes to Mangueira. He's not Mr T.R. He's the guy who receives Mr T.R. You never actually spoke to him.'

'Hmm, I don't know. Do you really believe that?'

'What?'

'C'mon, do you really believe that?'

'Whether I believe or not is another story. I'm just explaining the logic of it to you.'

'But do you believe it?'

'I don't fucking know. I already told you. I like the idea that there's somebody protecting me, helping me, without necessarily asking for good behaviour in return, unconditional devotion. At least at the *terreiro* there's no priest telling me I'm going to hell for having a wank. I like the logic of Umbanda. Now, whether I believe it or not, I don't know. Usually I say I'm a bisexual of faith. I'm torn between atheism and Umbanda, I tell myself I like them both, when actually I only want one, but I refuse to admit which one.'

'You've had too much to drink. I can't handle this crap.'

Andréa struggled unsuccessfully to convince someone to leave with her. She didn't want to take a taxi by herself, so she told the others she couldn't stand the heat any more and was going to get some fresh air in the uncovered part of the courtyard.

She returned to the obstacle course of sweaty bodies and remembered she still hadn't made the offering requested by Mr T.R. Too hard to buy the seven black candles and the seven red candles. No time. She didn't really know where to find them on the way from home to work, in between Ipanema and Gávea. If she knew where to find them, she wouldn't know where to park her car. If she knew where to park her car, she wouldn't have time. Buying the candles was one of the tasks on her mental to-do list to be performed in a near future that never came, along with paying her overdue long-distance phone bill, taking the dress she'd worn to Flavinha's wedding to the cleaners, asking the doorman to hang the paintings in the apartment she'd moved into three months ago, those kinds of things. And if one day she finally did manage to buy the candles, she'd have to light them in front of a crossroads. That would be much harder. It would be making a commitment. And as impressed as she'd been by the presence of the Exu Tranca Rua das Almas at the *terreiro*, she didn't know if she was willing to commit to him. Therefore, taking the dress she'd worn to Flavinha's wedding to the cleaners would remain the priority on her list of insurmountable tasks.

The breeze from the street at the entrance to the *favela* carried a series of smells that weren't very pleasing, but also a certain relief to her lungs in contrast to the cloistered stuffiness felt in the courtyard's epicentre. Andréa felt comfortable enough to light a cigarette leaning against the railing, when she saw the Exu looking at her. 'Not the Exu, the horse', she thought, and smiled at him. Soon her spontaneity turned to embarrassment. Especially when she realised he wasn't just smiling back. He approached her.

Andréa observed the man: this time there was no bare chest sticking out from under a black velvet cape, just a white and green-printed shirt, a pair of white trousers and pale leather shoes – an accessory that under normal circumstances would be enough to banish a man from her life forever. Without the top hat, she could see that the man was verging on baldness, and appeared older than she'd thought, closer to his late forties than early. But his strong face, framed by the white beard, was still there.

'You're not enjoying the samba?' he asked.

'I just came to rest a bit,' Andréa replied, noticing that the tone, accent, rhythm, everything in that man's voice was different than the one she'd heard at the *terreiro*.

'Are you here alone, Miss?'

'No, I'm here with a bunch of friends.'

'I know. But are you with your boyfriend?'

Andréa laughed.

'May I offer you a beer?'

Andréa laughed again. Over the next hour, she was amused to see that whole intimidating demeanour of the Exu now giving way, on the same face, to seductive bows that exuded a somewhat antiquated gentlemanly ritual – something she had already been accustomed to seeing among the older men who frequented samba circles and samba school rehearsals – as well as a masculine insecurity that surprised and touched her compared to the image of the exploding gun powder. Over the next hour, she learned a little about the horse's life: his name was Roberto, divorced, father of two, state government employee, and resident of the District of Fátima. At his insistence, she convinced herself to move onto the dance floor, but not without voicing her shame for not knowing how to samba. When her friends came to get her to leave, she didn't hesitate to give her phone number to Roberto, even though she knew that shortly thereafter, at Cervantes, they would take the piss out of her for reciprocating the flirtations of an older man.

In the three dates they had in two weeks, Roberto never let Andréa open her purse. As much as she found this old-fashioned chivalry charming, she would rather have contributed some money, at least to enable them to do it in a love hotel with clean sheets, and not some fleapit on Rua do Senado. Despite the disappointments, she couldn't say no to an invitation from him.

Andréa kept these dates secret. She hadn't told the friend who introduced her to the *terreiro* for fear of bringing him into some ethical debate. Wouldn't sleeping with the horse of the spirit be the same as screwing your psychoanalyst? Or worse? Because if it were psychoanalysis, the most dramatic consequence would be for the professional, who could lose his license if reported. Something she would never do. The farthest she usually went with taking revenge on a former lover was publicising his penile inadequacies.

But by sleeping with Roberto she could be infringing a code of ethics subject to forces she didn't even believe in, but knew to be stronger than her. From the first night with Roberto, she tried not to think about it. But she wasn't always successful.

When she heard the moans of a couple of cats in heat under her window, she frightened herself with the idea it was a warning and immediately searched for a sleeping pill. When she felt a cold shiver passing in front of a church, she took a sleeping pill when she got back home. When her bag was stolen by a boy on a bicycle, she needed a pill to sleep. For two weeks, Andréa had left all the lights on at home and went to sleep with a pill, after convincing her dermatologist friend to give her a prescription for Rivotril, claiming it was stress at work.

The fear of possible punishment for acting against principles she didn't know was therefore easily and chemically manageable. At this point, what disturbed Andréa when she recognised Roberto's office number on her mobile was something else. It was her guaranteed dissatisfaction.

On answering the phone, she would accept his invitation to 'have a beer', a euphemism for 'an hour and a half of dull conversation until the man thinks sufficient time has passed to suggest going to a hotel without looking like a scumbag'. Arriving at the hotel, she would let out a sigh when she saw the poorly made bed with threadbare baby pink sheets on a mattress covered in fake leather, doubly troubled by seeing her expression of dismay in the mirrors that lined the walls. As usual.

Andréa wanted to be everywhere, because she never wanted to be anywhere. If she actually thought about it, she would realise that she didn't even want to be in her own body. On those nights with Roberto, however, it was different. She knew she didn't want to be there, but she knew for certain where she did want to be: at a place with a dirt floor, the scent of gunpowder and a continuous drumbeat in the background.

Yes, the muscular torso and grey beard were attractive to her, but it wasn't Roberto who turned her on.

With other men, she had felt the gap between physical

and intellectual attraction. With herself, she had felt the gap between her own self and the shell she wore. But not like it was there, in that simple hotel, on threadbare baby pink sheets, that she imagined had once been red.

She insisted on dim lighting and when Robert penetrated her, she avoided the mirrors and looked at her lover's face, squinting her eyes, intentionally creating a blurry image of the man on top of her so she could fill in the empty spaces with carnivalesque props: a top hat, a cape. For the first time in her not very deep sexual experience, she achieved orgasm with penetration. And anticipating the possibility of orgasm, even considering that Roberto didn't move inside her with a rhythm that pleased her, the same Andréa, who moments earlier had demanded her partner use a condom, allowed herself be carried away by the fantasy of being impregnated. Impregnated by an entity who brought her feelings of fear and protection in equal measure, a spirit she had been taught to disdain in catechism classes, a being that transformed her into an anti-Mary, raising her to a supernatural order much more complete and complex than her own life. In that brief moment of orgasm, Andréa didn't want to be anywhere else but her own body.

Her problem came next: the disappointment of seeing there was only Roberto on top of her.

The boy, dizzy from glue, had a crust of snot that ran from both nostrils and met in the space between the nose and the central portion of his lips. Andréa wondered if there was a name for this part of the body; so small, so insignificant, that eventually turned into a telltale repository for bad habits. She gritted her teeth, not just in disgust for the boy, but also for the memory of when she had spent an entire evening snorting cocaine and barely realised that there, in the same area, a crust of blood and white powder had formed. Distracted by her thoughts, she didn't realise Roberto had bought a rose from the boy until he handed her the flower. It was wilted, wrapped in transparent paper affixed with a small red bow at the base, like all the roses sold by street vendors. She accepted the rose uneasily, noticing it was wilted and tacky, and her embarrassment progressed to stress on seeing the smile on Roberto's face. It was not the first time a man offered her a rose from a street vendor, but it was the first time a man had done it with no irony intended.

She had already lost count of her dates with Roberto at Amarelinho da Glória restaurant. Seven, maybe eight. For her it was the perfect place: little chance of being seen by someone she knew and close to the hotel on Rua do Senado. The wilted rose didn't mark much of a change to their routine, but Roberto's smile was yet another sign of something that Andréa had been noticing and that frightened her. Roberto's gallantry, initially just the ritual of a man delighted to be going out with a pretty, well-dressed young woman from Gávea, seemed increasingly imbued with something that Andréa... no, she wasn't sure, she couldn't be sure, but it was something that Andréa increasingly perceived as sincerity. She wouldn't dare tell herself that Roberto was in love. She wouldn't know how to recognise the signals from someone almost twice her age and from such a distant cultural universe. But it was clear that Roberto already saw a relationship there. In the beginning they just made clumsy conversation before getting in the taxi to Rua do Senado. But lately, as soon as they got to the bar, he'd give her a kiss on the lips, instead of two kisses on the cheek. Sitting there, he spent almost the entire time with his hand on Andréa's hand, which led her to smoke more, as the moment she used both hands to hold the lighter and cigarette was her only respite. This time, she had arrived late, and Roberto had saved her a chair next to his. Yes, next to his. Not across from him, with the table imposing a respectful distance. Next to him, with their thighs touching, like boyfriend and girlfriend. And after the rose, came the worst part: he suggested a date at the weekend. On Saturday night! He asked her to go with him – with him, mind you, not to meet him there – to the Mangueira samba rehearsal.

Andréa replied that she would check her schedule and call to confirm. She didn't want to go. She didn't want to be with him anymore. But she couldn't get out of it so easily. She couldn't conceive of abandoning the orgasm, the moment she felt herself being possessed by Exu in the flesh, even though the reality check that followed left her deeply dissatisfied.

There were four days of hesitation, placated by the tablets at bedtime. She avoided leaving the house and answering the phone, she didn't want to meet anyone so as not to risk revealing her dilemma over a bar table. And when Roberto called, on Saturday afternoon, as agreed, Andréa said yes, she would go to Mangueira with him. She hadn't reached her decision. She just blurted out yes, on the spot.

At the rehearsal she ventured her *gringa* samba steps with Roberto, drank the beers he brought her, let friends and acquaintances see her exchanging kisses with him. To hell with it. To hell with that group of posh kids from Posto 9 who come to the *favela* and don't mingle with the locals. She'd taken on a new confidence that night, partly from having had three shots of vodka earlier, at home. There, seeing Roberto proudly showing her off to his friends, watching his mastery of the samba steps, Andréa was sure she had made the right decision, even though she'd made it on impulse. And she became even more sure of it when Roberto whispered: 'Let's go to my place' in her ear, leaving her quivering with desire.

When they arrived at the apartment in Fátima, she felt relief to see it was bigger than she imagined, and just as devoid of taste as she imagined. She threw herself on the sofa with him as soon as he produced two cans of beer from the fridge, listening to noises from the bats in the almond trees on the street. She felt his moistened beard scratch her lips, felt his rough hand slip between her thighs, her knickers, her labia, and she asked:

'Do you have your cape here?'

Though taken aback, Roberto didn't stop fondling her clitoris:

'What?'

'Your cape. Your top hat. I'd like you to receive the Tranca-Rua for us to shag.'

Roberto's hand hovered motionless for a few seconds then started to back up: his fingers escaped from under her knickers and walked down her right thigh toward her knee, until it was freed from the skirt and, finally, of any contact with Andréa.

'Is that what you want?' he asked, breathing deeply, heavily.

'Yes, yes,' said Andréa, stroking the hair on his chest with her hands.

'It's not going to happen.'

'Why not? Just this once?'

Roberto then asked Andréa to leave. A gentleman, he offered to accompany her down to Rua do Riachuelo, and put her in the taxi. The walk down the hill was made in total silence, punctuated only by Andréa's questions, which were met with more silence by Roberto. 'Did I do something wrong?' 'Did I offend you?' 'I didn't know you couldn't, forgive me!?' The only one to get a reply was: 'Did you not remember that I'd gone to the *terreiro*?'

'I remembered. Not in the beginning, I think it was the third or fourth time I saw you. Sometimes we remember a few things. But I never imagined that was why you were with me.'

Andréa cried on the taxi ride home. She didn't really understand what was happening. She cried from embarrassment, the most pure and simple embarrassment of someone who puts herself forward and gets rejected. By the time she arrived home she had already moved on to being angry with herself.

When she got out of the shower, she'd reached the stage of feeling sorry for herself. As she looked for the bottle of sleeping pills, she thought she would wake up early on Monday morning and go downtown before work. She wanted to stop by an Umbanda shop on Marechal Floriano, an address her friend had given her and that she'd jotted down days ago on the notepad next to the phone. She would buy the black and red candles for the offering.

When she swallowed the pill, she thought she could make the most of her trip and also buy a top hat and black velvet cape. Maybe at some point she would meet someone.

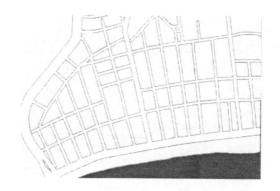

I Love You

Patrícia Melo

Translated by Daniel Hahn

I ASK, HE answers, I speak, he asks, I answer, he asks again, speaks again, speaks slowly, he thinks about saying something, but nothing is said, nothing's revealed. It doesn't look like there's any hurry. Where are we going? I want to know.

He's sweating, he's nervous. I'm getting more and more uncomfortable. I ask if the police will be getting mixed up with this, or weapons or drugs or anything illegal.

Don't worry about it, he reassures me.

I don't like any dirty stuff, I warn him. Not threesomes, either.

He smiles and says nor does he.

And I don't like drugs, I insist.

Dani keeps sending me these text messages: *Where have you got to? We're doing our nails. I've done mine bright blue. We're at home getting ready. We're going dancing at Demo.* And the two of us driving round the neighbourhood, and now here's this guy telling me all I have to do is agree with him. Agree with what? I ask. With whatever I say, he answers. He says, Imagine it's like in a theatre, we're going to arrive, we'll ring the bell, a woman will answer, we'll give a little performance, that's what we're going to do, like in the theatre, I'll talk to her, maybe we'll argue a little, and all you're going to do is just agree with whatever I say.

The whole business had begun badly. He only had to say, 'My name is W.', and that was it, he'd been identified and

101

labelled: stark raving mad. Card-carrying member of the loonies' club and everything. *I'm so screwed, Dani, I can't answer now, let me know when you get to Demo.* To tell the truth, even much earlier when W. called me for the first time and said he'd seen my website, I sensed something rotten in the state of Denmark. *Where are you, wild girl?* There's a particular kind of square, who wears his shirt tucked into his trousers, and shoes with gold buckles just the same as the executives and businessmen I go with, but who's got a *je ne sais quoi* that gets my guard up right away, I'm terrified of going out with some bastard murderer and being discovered strangled in a motel. The worst kind of shame, dying like that. *Man, I'm doing some uni work, don't know if I'll be able to get out, when you get to Demo let me know if Tito's there.* Are you really nineteen? Do you really speak English? Could you tie your hair back? And remove your make-up? How can you type those numbers so quickly on your phone? Who's sending you so many messages? Do you have a boyfriend?

What the hell does this guy want from me, with his machinegun-fire of questions? My answers are as good as his; in this business you quickly learn how to pretend. Telling the truth is for beginners.

No sooner had I arrived at his house, where there were piles and piles of algebra books and a monster Saint Bernard hibernating in one corner, than he asked me, after offering me some wine, whether I really was a psychology student. Do you want to test me on my Freud? I asked. He didn't even laugh. *Demo rocking. Everyone here. Gabizinha, Bel, Lia, Ka, Dedé, Sofi, Nina, Paulinha, even annoying Nat is here with her skanky cousin, that stressed-out one from São Paulo who argued with Gi about splitting the cab fare LOL.*

Here it is, he says, parking the car outside a building on Venâncio Flores. Nothing to be afraid of, it'll be quick, he says.

We take the lift up in silence. *Is Tito there? Please, Dani, pretty-please tell me if he shows up.* Remember, he says before we step out onto the eighth floor, you just have to keep quiet and agree with whatever I say.

We ring the bell and this old lady about his age, early forties, opens the door. I can tell three things about her at a glance: she works out a lot, she drinks a lot and has a smoker's rasp.

Hi Marta, he says.

Marta tuts, and jams herself into the doorway, forcing us to stay out in the hall.

Him: I said I'd bring her. Satisfied now?

Her: What are you talking about?

Him: Don't pretend you don't understand.

Dani: Tito's friends are all here. Betão's had a haircut. Looks ridiculous!

Another tut from Marta. From the living-room, the sound of a television, a reporter saying that six thousand one hundred and seventy-eight people die in the world every hour.

Him: She's my lover, Marta.

Her: Ah! I get it.

Me: Ask Betão about Tito.

Now the announcer is saying that there are a hundred and forty-eight thousand two hundred and sixty two deaths per day. Is that all? I'm interested.

Him: I'm telling you, she's my lover!

Her: Keep your voice down. I'm not deaf.

Reporter: Four thousand from lack of water, twenty-four thousand of hunger.

Him: You're the one who's shouting, you lunatic.

Me: Wouldn't it be better if we went in?

They both agree.

Dani: Listen up, folks – drumroll, please: Tito is coming.

Now we go into the apartment, which is crammed full of trinkets and cushions and picture-frames, with a number of photos of the couple in India, on the Xingu. The two of them have done a lot of travelling. For a moment the three of us just stand there, awkwardly, in front of the sofa, like martial arts fighters who've just been pulled apart by the referee and who now need to be rearranged into a position that looks like it's something out of the Kama Sutra. Finally the two of them resume their argument.

Her: So, that's our reality now, is it? You ringing my doorbell and trying to persuade me you have a lover.

It occurs to me I oughtn't to have worn such high heels. If I'd known the night was going to be the kind that ends up in a freestyle wrestling-match I would have chosen my flats. Actually, had Dani even returned my flats? Can I sit down? I ask. *Dani, where are my red flats?*

Him: Aren't you my lover?

It takes me a moment to realise that the question is for me, and I reply clumsily, yes, of course, I'm your lover. Can I sit down?

Dani: Lol… wearing them now…

Him: Tell her we've been together for two years.

Me: We've been together for two years. Can I sit down?

Her: What's this kid saying?

Me: Tell her she's not to call me a kid again.

Him: She wants to sit down. That's all. Make yourself comfortable, sweetheart.

I sit down.

Me: Cheeky bitch. You're not going to wreck my lovely new flats.

Her: "Sweetheart"? What kind of idiot talk is "sweetheart"? This is my house, since when do you tell people to sit down?

I get up, I don't like this one bit.

Before I complain, she realises how rude she has been and apologises. She says I'm not the one she has a problem with but that "idiot man" and that I can indeed sit down.

I sit down. Then, appraising me as though she were the owner of a modeling agency, Marta says to W. what is blatantly obvious: that he doesn't even know me.

Her: So what's your name then?

Me: Fernanda.

Her: You are not this cretin's lover. For one simple reason: you're intelligent. Anyone who looks at you, Fernanda, knows that you – beautiful the way you are and so smart – wouldn't look twice at this jungle-pig.

I smile. W. feigns a burst of laughter, but really the guy has absolutely no talent for lying.

Her: OK, so the game is to cause trouble, then. So let's do it. I'm good at this, too. If you're this idiot's lover, tell me: which day was he born?

Him: I forbid you to answer, Fernanda. This lady is sick.

Dani: Tito's just arrived.

Her: I knew it. You and your tricks.

Him: I don't care whether you believe me or not, Marta. I just came here to introduce you to my lover. That's all.

Me: Where's the bathroom?

Her: Now she wants to go to the bathroom.

Him: Your problem, Marta, is that you want to be unhappy. You won't accept having a man who loves you and who wants what's best for you. You want me to have cancer? A heart attack?

Somehow or other I've got to call Dani. I've got to find out about Tito.

Me: May I use your bathroom, Marta?

Marta: Tell your lover she's not to speak my name.

Him: You believe me now?

Me: I really do need to go to the toilet.

Her: Your problem is that you're a chronic liar. You're a son of a bitch. I saw your phone bill and I know exactly what you've been up to.

Dani: Tito is goooorgeous! And on his own. Shit, he's coming over to talk to me.

Me: I need to go to the bathroom, I tell the two of them.

Him: So I'm the guilty one now, am I? Marta? Me? I do everything you want. Even that piece of shit in Búzios, I only bought that to make you happy. And what about you? What do you do? You nose around in my things. For fuck's sake, Marta. For fuck's sake. Marta. For fuck's sake. You're a piece of work. For fuck's sake. Even my phone bill?

I leave the pair of them arguing and find the toilet on my own. I call Dani and she doesn't pick up.

Out there the two of them are like a broken record. For fuck's sake, Marta. Marta. For fuck's sake. You this. You that.

Me: Don't do this to me, Dani! Pick up, wild girl.

Nothing. Damn it, what's going on? Could Dani be chatting Tito up? I'm going to kill Dani.

Me: Daniiiiiiiiiiiiiiiiii! Fuck's sake. What's going on?

Nothing. Out there, I hear it really kicking off. She cries. Shouts. He asks, she doesn't answer, she asks, he shouts, she shouts louder, they both shout. And then complete silence.

They must have killed each other, I think. I look in the mirror, I look dreadful. Bags under my eyes. And this horrible spot on my forehead. Imagine Tito seeing me with this spot.

Me: Dani, would you please answer me at once?!

Damn, what kind of fucking friend is Dani?

The silence coming from the two of them worries me. Uh-oh. Now they're nattering away again, is that it? Is it just my impression or does Marta really believe now that I'm W.'s lover?

I decide to put on some make-up. W. can go fuck himself. That's why I take the money right away on arrival. If anything goes wrong, I have my guarantee. Are they really going to be mewling like this all night?

Dani: Wait up, crazy girl. I couldn't answer in front of Tito. Tito's looking hot. Good news.

Me: About Tito? Tell me quickly.

I go back to the living-room and Marta is in tears. W. is beside her, desperate. When he sees me, he asks me to say it's all a lie.

You can tell the truth, Marta adds. Tell me, I can take it. Tell me. I know you're his lover. I can take it. Say it. Just stab me in the heart. I could expect anything of this man. He's ruined my life.

Him: For fuck's sake, Marta. Stop that. Marta, for fuck's sake, I love you, for fuck's sake.

Dani: Tito asked after you. Sounding interested. Come soon. He's got like a thousand utter slags hitting on him.

I want to jump for joy.

Me: Daninha, my gorgeous friend, warn Tito I'll be there soon, I'm on my way, I'm racing over.

Him: I don't even know this woman. You think I'd go out with someone like her?

Me: Wow – no, none taken...

Him: Sorry, what I meant was, you're young, I could be your father. But I don't even know you, do I?

Her: You swear?

Me: It's the honest truth. I don't know your husband. I was hired.

Her: You went to an agency for help, pumpkin?

Him: We have to stop hurting each other, Marta. We have to put an end to this, baby.

As I step into the lift I can still hear Marta sobbing and W. saying over and over, 'For fuck's sake, I love you, for fuck's sake. Marta. For fuck's sake, Marta.'

I pull out my red lipstick and take advantage of the mirror to draw on a properly outrageous mouth. Now, time to race over to Demo. It's going to be a good night.

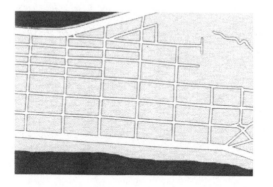

Places, in the Middle of Everything

Elvira Vigna

Translated by Lucy Greaves

THE WINDOWS OF those trendy shops display the tight, v-neck t-shirts they imagine are the trademark of successful, athletic young people. I guess they must think we're all like that, even those who lack success and have scant youth left. We're all the same to them. Those young people represent our true 'I'. They're the shadow that follows us everywhere, flaunting their colours and their biceps, while we walk the streets, alone, flabby and unhappy. But we know full well that this isn't how we are either. We're the thing that accompanies us, furtively. Yes, we do have biceps, and washboard stomachs, in this other version of ourselves that isn't quite our opposite: it's our true 'us' which puts on this shabby, decrepit show just for fun. Because we haven't the time to take on our true form: the shop window mannequin. After all, it's a beach city, we're all athletic here. Perhaps because we have no choice. And everything is geared towards athletic types: marketing, personal and social expectations, any kind of plan for the future.

I even think I once bought a t-shirt from this very shop, back when I still gave presents or still believed there were people I might give presents to. I asked for the t-shirt to be wrapped in shiny paper, even though it was on sale and I had to pay more for the shiny paper. The fabric was pretty poor quality, but there was a picture of a surfer on the front. The

111

present was for a small, thin man who used to stay on the beach for days on end, talking like a surfer or how he imagined – and we all imagined – surfers talked. He'd been my husband once, back when you could stay at the beach until six, when the waves were always blue, with surfers and islands in the distance.

I have no idea if it's the same shop. And, in fact, I only remembered it after I'd sat down on the step outside and began to search for some kind of intimacy, invented even, with the place I'd chosen to temporarily accommodate my bum. It was good, sitting there on the step. I could feel slight gusts from the air conditioning inside, and there was sufficient distance between me and the ground. But it's easy to mistake one shop for another: they're all so alike, selling clothes or other stuff. So I don't know.

There were some roadworks on the street that I hadn't noticed when I sat down. We'd rather not notice roadworks: we'd rather not admit that in fact nothing will ever be finished. But the drilling starts up again. In front of me, beyond the shoals of jeans and trainers swimming past at eye level, is the café where one day you sat to wait for your lover. I find myself at the exact spot on the pavement where she, approaching from your left and rounding the corner, still on the other side (my side) of the road, would have been able to see you before you saw her. The Leblon café, along with everything that followed and everything that went before, that finally made us go our separate ways. It was for the best, in your opinion.

I glance over at the café. It's just a glance, but it helps to anchor me. Sitting low down, on the step in front of the shop, I'm at almost the same level as the smartly set little table with its three empty chairs; it's still early and the place is empty. I am she; my gaze is superimposed on your lover's, resting on an empty chair which I fill with movements and details I didn't see. In the absence of such images I resort to scenes from French films, which are also more imagined than remembered. What I'm calling the present moment, for want of a better phrase, is therefore an absence, a radical one.

I don't simply sit and look at what isn't there, at a time that isn't now, with eyes that aren't mine. In order to stay where I am without being moved on by the round man in a black suit who drifts back and forth, like a kite at the mercy of the breeze or, at least, the air conditioning gusting through the door, I rely on my appearance, which isn't really mine either. It belongs to any old twin sister, one I invented a long time ago. And who, in gutters and on the steps outside shops, on dirty, decaying benches in squares, perched awkwardly on fire hydrants and curbstones, imitates clothes and roars of laughter long since forgotten, along with definitions of who I am that I can no longer trust. My twin still wears clothes which, despite my battered old shoes, lend me a slight air of bourgeois dignity. They serve as a barrier between me and, for example, the shop's security guard who takes a step towards me then hesitates. He should move me on, but I look slightly richer than anticipated.

I don't want to move from this spot. I pull my mobile out of my pocket. I frown, pretending to concentrate on the small illuminated screen, I type important messages, I press different keys, I say a stern 'hello' to no one, before snapping it shut, fixing my gaze on the cosmic nothing as if I were an important person pondering important business. And I keep my mobile in my hand: it's my weapon. Look, I've got a mobile. You can't move me on. People with electronic devices don't get moved on. But after this scene between me and the shop's security guard, the café table with its three chairs seems a bit further away.

It's a bit further away in time as well. If I saw you there now, you too would be your own twin. Because you chose a new you as well, one in which you feel more at ease, your clothes hanging more loosely over your greasy stomach. A you that's more in keeping with the life you now lead, the life that exists since our negotiations drew to a close.

I get a warning from my knees or my feet, I don't know which, either way they've gone to sleep: I need to stretch my legs out. I need to move, but if I do, the bits of me that I said were my twin's will be lost again, and they're the best bits. Not because they're intrinsically better, but because they get lost from time to time. My bum's sore as well as my legs. The step, impersonal as it is, refuses to emulate our wicker sofa, which moulded itself to my body and yours, an opposite 'us', a negative of us – in more than one sense – waiting for us to get our nightly television fix. I stand up. I need to eat something. Not that I'm really hungry. The thing is, I don't have a present moment, but that doesn't mean I can't see into the future. I'll be sweating again in a few minutes, cold this time. And a few minutes after that I'll be on the verge of fainting. Low blood pressure, everyone will say, and I'll be with them. Sure, OK, low blood pressure, hypoglycaemia, an empty stomach or whatever. The little card someone gave me, for a 'natural' restaurant, already found its way into the bin dozens of metres back.

You already called me, I know that without having to look: I felt the vibration in my hand. The silent mobile vibrated and I kept it closed, preferring just the vibration. It vibrates even harder than the drill, telling me that, finally, here I am.

You're going to ask me how my morning was. I'm going to describe my footnotes and leave out the main text.

You've got that kind of van thing. You open the bonnet and offer – instead of bread, cakes and cheeses – attention, politeness, subtle consideration. In return, so that it stays parked in the same place (close to me), you expect more potent, spontaneous flavours. You think it's a fair deal. And I'll fill it up with this torrent of words that you don't want to hear, as if with adulterated petrol. In the end, you'll pause respectfully before trying to change the subject, not realising that it's exactly the same subject: death and the ridiculous remnants left behind by any death. The smell of an expensive old perfume, almost worn-out brown leather bags, used towels. A comb that still holds a strand of hair, like a worm moving through hardened air, stuck fast in death's cement-like air, impossible to remove. I'll go back to the guessed-invented-memories of you in the café which are alive, like all films.

But, even so, I return your call.

In the taxi we seem like marathon runners, at least from the waist up. Sweat pours down our faces, and we overtake buildings and people, lampposts and dogs on either side. There's no sound in this world of ours; the car windows are closed. The driver turned on the air-conditioning and is struggling to make headway, but he knows, just as we do, that we're going from A to B, yet A and B are one and the same – and nowhere. But that isn't what matters: the important thing is to just keep running. It rained briefly at the end of the afternoon and that was probably what did it. The rain sent me back to my B-movie, where it's always dark and rainy. Although there aren't always lovers in cafés. We stopped for something to eat.

I stared at the wet asphalt, the puddles and, in them, the lights of buses and cars. I thought it could be one of those so-called special moments. I was leaning just the way I like to, half my back resting against the bar, the other half against the back of the high stool. I don't always get it right. The edge of the bar was digging into my ribs a bit. It was better lower down. I'd been walking all day, so my legs were glad to be still. I waited for the special moment. It's not difficult. You look into the distance, take in noises that you're actually listening to without noticing. And everything else slots into a meaning that you know exists, even though you struggle to say what it is. It's not really a meaning. It's more a sense that a meaning does exist. And then you pause, and your face looks more intelligent than usual. And that's what I thought could happen. But beside me, you were eating. I'd already finished; you were finishing your Big Bim *bauru*. We were in Big Bim

Snacks. The Big Bim *bauru* is the best sandwich you can get at Big Bim Snacks. Steak, bread, lettuce, tomato. Chips. You finished it. You ordered another one. That spoiled things a bit. Beside you, a guy was carefully eating a chicken drumstick. He put ketchup on it. The big blobs, which struggled to escape from the little plastic pillow those things come in now, gave a sense of high drama entirely absent from your second Big Bim.

You ate half and stopped, your mouth slightly open.

'It shouldn't have happened.'

I thought about nodding my head to say yes, I knew. But I didn't. You looked at me for a while longer and then carried on. Starting with the chips. Grabbing a chip with your hand and shoving it furiously into your mouth was a kind of answer to my non-answer, one that worked better (you must have thought, and I agree with you) than grabbing the steak sandwich and trying to bite into it, which might or might not do the trick. There are times when the steak comes out whole, when your teeth aren't sharp enough to cut through it. And that would completely ruin the conversation.

But things calmed down a bit after that. You were already on your second or third chip from the second plate and, gradually, eating the chip became just that, eating a chip and not an answer to my non-answer.

But you had to mark the end of the scene. You wiped your mouth.

'I'll say it as many times as I have to: it shouldn't have happened.'

This time I looked at you.

Up until then I was still in my B-movie, in the puddles, in the buses, and bemoaning the fact that it was only eight in the evening, lots of people hurrying home, kids, shopping. I looked at you because, in some way, the B-movie wasn't really going that well. I wanted to say something completely unconnected. Like, hurry up because somethings going to happen. Or tomorrow you'll be doing something. I couldn't think of anything. So I just sat there looking at you.

It wasn't cold. But I knew that when I moved, when I uncrossed my legs to recross them the other way, the skin that had been pressing against the other patch of skin would now feel cold because it was exposed to the air. I uncrossed them anyway. It was a mistake. That movement stripped all intensity from the scene. You went back to eating.

At some point, looking over the counter at the line of avocados neatly arranged beneath the bananas and grapes, I said:

'I know.'

The waitress had put on weight. I didn't recognise her at first. I needed to recover my memory of her while she was standing there before me. Back then they used to do something we thought was a lot of fun. We used to have to pay at the till. And if, after paying, we went back to the bar to leave a tip, whoever picked up the money would shout, really loud:

'Tip!'

Or, in our case, because you always liked to give bigger tips than you'd expect from people who looked as scruffy as us:

'Fat tip!'

At which all the employees, even if they were behind the wall of fruit, in that small space that passed for a kitchen, would shout, in unison:

'Thank you!'

Really loud.

And we would walk out, laughing, into the street; the street never changed. It's just the same now, more often than not damp from the rain that always falls so suddenly in this city. And, holding hands, we would go – as we will in a few minutes – over to the cheap hotel across the road, where the noise of the air conditioning would mask my moans. Because I never worried about being discreet, even when our room is, like it is this time, the closest to the lift and, therefore, closest to the ears of whoever is waiting – always for ages – for the old, slow lift.

And there are always lots of people. Because there are lots of rooms. Because we used to go to that hotel even when we still lived in the city and we wanted to be alone, or just fancied a change of bed.

You, I thought without looking, must have already finished your second sandwich and the chips. I felt you touch my arm, calling me back to you with a look I was able to guess without turning on my high stool, without leaning away from the curve of the bar and the backrest.

I considered my options.

I could look at the puddles again. My B-movie was getting more convincing by the minute. Later that night, the sounds would get deeper, the flip-flops more pungent, the clientele more urgent – and more interesting. And the smells pervading the café, whether of food or deodorant under arms raised to order a bowl of *açaí*,[9] would get worse.

It was one option, and it was probably the one I should have gone for.

Or, second option, I would get down from the high stool at a given moment and say Bye, see you, knowing that you couldn't follow me, not immediately. You had to pay the bill first. While you settled up, I would fade into the shadow of the first building I came across, slip onto the first bus with an open door.

It would be good. Although, of course, no one disappears. Nothing disappears. Everything and everyone carries on forever, getting steadily slower, fatter, more boring, more washed-out, but carrying on nonetheless.

Even me.

Then I thought about just pretending I was going into my B-movie.

I could turn and look outside at the puddles, the buses, the passers-by, but with tears in my eyes. Eyes brimming over. That always makes for a good ending. A tear-filled ending cut

9. A dark red berry from a Brazilian palm of the same name.

short and that's that, all set for the new day.

But I couldn't be bothered.

I looked at your plate. You'd actually finished the second Big Bim. Then I said:

'Let's go.'

And you went to pay.

You didn't leave a tip. You must have forgotten.

Anyway, the girl on the till wouldn't say 'thank you' so loudly. She looked less lesbian and less interesting after all those years we'd spent away. It wouldn't be the same.

We started off towards the hotel. Your skin was hot and it warmed me when you hugged me. We were treading in my B-movie puddles while you were hugging me, which messed up sequences and zooms.

It's good to walk with legs that are tired from hardly moving. With your head quiet from almost not existing. It feels nice, I know that. You were kind of drunk, or you had been, and that must have been why you ordered the second Big Bim, to counter the effects of the cheap wine you said was really good, a real find, and drank almost all of by yourself, on the threadbare sofa of the house that, until today, could still be called Molly's house. And which, as of tomorrow, furniture down the stairs, doors wide open, walls showing marks that were previously hidden, will no longer have any name at all.

You're going to have a shower, then I will too. When I come out, wrapped in a towel, you'll be waiting for me in bed, your dick semi-hard. We know this script. It's always good. Afterwards, you'll be in a better mood, affectionate, as we flick through the few television channels they have in this hotel. You'll imagine it's all behind us and maybe, with time, I might forget. And you'll smile when I look at you as if looking at a stranger, not noticing that I'm looking at you as if looking at a stranger.

About the Authors

João Ximenes Braga was born in Rio in 1970 and is an author, journalist, and award-winning screenwriter. He has published four books including two novels, *Porra* ('Damn') and *Juízo* ('Judgement'), a short story collection, *A Mulher que Transou com o Cavalo e Outras Histórias* ('The Woman who Slept with the Horse and Other Stories'), and a collection of articles, *A Dominatrix Gorda* ('The Fat Dominatrix'). Since 2005 he has worked in television. *Lado a Lado* ('Side by Side'), co-written with Claudia Lage, his first telenovela as a main writer, received a 2013 International Emmy Award.

Cesar Cardoso was born in Rio de Janeiro in 1955 and is an author, poet and humourist, as well as a writer for TV, including the programmes *TV Pirata* ('TV Pirate'), *A Grande Família* ('The Big Family'), and the sitcom *Sai de Baixo* ('Get Out of the Way'). He has published three books with children's publisher Biruta. Other books include *Capoeira Camará*, *Você Pensa Que Água é H2O?* ('You Thought Water Was H2O?'), and the short story collection *As Primeiras Pessoas* ('The First People'). His stories have also featured in numerous anthologies.

Nei Lopes was born in Irajá in 1942. A former attorney, and professional composer (particularly of samba music), Lopes is renowned for his civil rights activism and, since 1981, has published several books, articles and essays on the subject, including the *Brazilian Encyclopaedia of the African Diaspora*. In the 1980s, Lopes was one of the supporters of the Pagode movement, which brought samba back to the airwaves. As an established songwriter, he has recorded and performed versions of his own songs as well as those of other composers.

Toni Marques (editor) was born in Rio in 1964 and is a former New York correspondent for *O Globo* newspaper (2000-2003), and a story editor for *Fantastico* (since 2007). He is currently the curator of FLUPP – the first and only international literary festival hosted by shanty town communities in Brazil. He has published four books; two of his short stories have been published in French by Éditions Anacaona.

Patrícia Melo was born in 1962 and is a highly-regarded novelist, playwright and scriptwriter. Prizes for her work include the Jabuti Prize, the Prix Fémina for the best foreign novel, the German LiBeraturpreis 2013, and the German Crime Award 2014. *Time* magazine included her among their '50 Latin American Leaders of the New Millennium'. Her novels have been shortlisted for the IMPAC award (2006), and the IFFP (2003). Germany's *Die Zeit* magazine chose *The Body Snatcher* as its best crime novel of 2013.

Marcelo Moutinho was born in Rio in 1972. A writer and journalist, he is the author of three short story collections – *A Palavra Ausente* ('The Absent Word', Rocco, 2011), *Somos Todos Iguais Nesta Noite* ('Tonight We are All the Same', Rocco, 2006), *Memória dos Barcos* ('Memories of Boats', 7Letras, 2001) – and the children's book *A Menina que Perdeu as Cores* ('The Girl who Lost her Colours', Pallas, 2013). He has edited several anthologies including *Dicionário Amoroso da Língua Portuguesa* ('Amorous Dictionary of the Portuguese Language', Casa da Palavra, 2009). He writes a weekly column for the online magazine *Vida Breve*, as well as several newspapers, including *O Globo*.

João Gilberto Noll was born in Porto Alegre in 1946 and is the author of nineteen books. His first collection of short stories, *O Cego e a Dançarina* ('The Blind Man and the Dancer') was published in 1980 and won three literary prizes.

His story included here, 'Something Urgently', was the basis for the film *Nunca Fomos Tão Felizes* (*Happier Than Ever*, 1983), directed by Murilo Salles and starring Claudio Marzo and Roberto Bataglin. Noll's recent works include the novel *Lorde* ('Lord', 2004), and the short story collections *Mínimos Múltiplos Comuns* ('Minimum Common Multiples', 2003) and *A Máquina de Ser* ('The Machine of Being', 2006). He has won more than ten literary awards, including the Jabuti Prize five times. His novel *Harmada* made *Bravo!* magazine's list of 100 essential Brazilian books of all time.

Domingos Pellegrini was born in Londrina in 1949 and writes short stories, novels, poetry and YA fiction. From a young age, he heard many stories told by the customers in his father's barber shop and his mother's guest-house. After graduating as an arts student, and working as a journalist, he published his first collection of short stories in 1977, *O Homem Vermelho* ('The Red Man'), which earned him the prestigious Jabuti Prize. That same year, he published a second short story collection, *Os Meninos* ('The Boys'). Other works of note include *Terra Vermelha* ('Red Land'), a colonial history of Paraná, and the novel *O Caso da Chácara Chão* ('The Case of the Country Bungalow'), which also received the Jabuti Prize.

Luiz Ruffato was born in Minas Gerais in 1961. He studied journalism at the Federal University of Juiz de Fora and made his debut as a novelist in 2001 with *Eles Eram Muitos Cavalos* ('There were Many Horses'), which received the Machado de Assis National Library Prize and the Paulista Arts Critics Prize. Ruffato has also published *De Mim Já Nem Se Lembra* ('They No Longer Remember Me', 2007), *Estive em Lisboa e Lembrei de Você* ('I Was in Lisbon and was Reminded of You', 2009), and the *Inferno Provisório* ('Provisional Hell') project, which is made up of five volumes and studies the development of the Brazilian proletariat from the 1950s to 2000. Prizes include the Jabuti Prize, the Brazilian Book Chamber Prize, and the Cuban Casa de las América Prize.

Sérgio Sant'Anna was born in Rio de Janeiro in 1941 and has written novels, several volumes of short stories, and plays. His career as a writer began in the 1960s with the foundation of *Estória*, a magazine for experimental literature, which was later banned during the military dictatorship. In the 1970s he was part of Brazil's literary avant-garde, which attempted to link experimental literary forms with revolutionary commitment. For several years, Sant'Anna was a lecturer in communication science at the University of Rio de Janeiro. His work has been awarded the Jabuti Prize four times.

Katie Slade (editor) graduated from Manchester Metropolitan University in 2013 with an MA in Creative Writing. She has worked at Comma Press since 2011.

Elvira Vigna was born in Rio de Janeiro in 1947 and began her literary career as a writer of fiction for children and young people, until she published *Sete Anos e Um Dia* ('Seven Years and A Day'), her first novel for adults. She runs a translation agency and practises as a visual artist. Her art work has been exhibited in numerous venues around Rio, including the Gávea Planetarium (1996), and the Vila Riso (1998). She has also worked as a magazine cover artist, and has been a prolific journalist since the 1990s, writing for *O Globo*, *Folha de São Paulo*, and *Jornal do Brazil*. To date, she has published 34 books including novels, short stories and theoretical works.

About the Translators

Ana Fletcher is a translator and editor. She holds a BA in English from the University of York and an MA in Comparative Literature from UCL. Her translations of short stories and poetry by contemporary Lusophone writers have been published in *Granta*, *Music & Literature* and *Wasafiri* magazines. Ana can also be found editing literary fiction for the independent publishing house And Other Stories. Born and raised in Lisbon, she now lives in Rio de Janeiro.

Lucy Greaves translates from Portuguese, Spanish and French and was awarded the 2013 Harvill Secker Young Translators' Prize. She has been one of the Free Word Centre's two Translators in Residence during 2014. Her translations of Eliane Brum's *One, Two* and Mamen Sánchez's *Happiness is a Cup of Tea with You* are forthcoming in late 2014 and early 2015 respectively, and her work has been published by Granta and *Words Without Borders*, among others.

Daniel Hahn is a writer, editor and translator with some forty books to his name. His translations from Portuguese, Spanish and French include fiction from Europe, Africa and the Americas, and non-fiction by writers ranging from a Portuguese Nobel laureate to Brazilian footballer, Pelé. He is currently compiling the new *Oxford Companion to Children's Literature*.

Kim M. Hastings is a freelance translator and editor based in the US. She lived in São Paulo for several years, studied Brazilian language and literature at Brown University, and holds a PhD in Spanish and Portuguese from Yale. Her translations include Edgard Telles Ribeiro's award-winning novel *His Own Man* as well as short fiction in magazines such as *Words Without Borders, Review: Literature and Arts of the Americas, Two Lines, Bookanista*, and *Machado de Assis*.

Amanda Hopkinson is Professor of Literary Translation at City University, London and was previously Director of the British Centre for Literary Translation (2004-2010). She translates from the Portuguese (José Saramago, Paulo Coelho); Spanish (Elena Poniatowska, Juan Villoro); and French (Dominique Manotti) – among other authors. She is also a Trustee of English PEN, *Modern Poetry in Translation,* and the Wales Literature Exchange.

Sophie Lewis is a London-born writer, editor and translator from French and Portuguese. Recent translations include *Thérèse and Isabelle* by Violette Leduc (Salammbô), *The Man Who Walked Through Walls* by Marcel Aymé (Pushkin) and *The Earth Turned Upside Down* by Jules Verne (Hesperus). She is principal editor at And Other Stories press, and moved to Rio de Janeiro in 2011.

Zoë Perry is a Canadian-American translator who grew up in rural south-eastern Kentucky. She completed a BA in French and International Studies at Guilford College and an MA in Intercultural Communication at Anglia Ruskin University. After living and working in Brazil for nearly four years, and for briefer periods in Portugal, France, Spain, and Russia, she is currently based in the UK. Her co-translation of Rodrigo de Souza Leão's *All Dogs are Blue* with Stefan Tobler was published in 2013 by And Other Stories.

Brazilian by birth, **Julia Sanches** has lived in New York, Mexico City, Lausanne, Edinburgh, and Barcelona. She was runner-up in *Modern Poetry in Translation*'s poetry translation competition and winner of the *SAND* journal translation competition and the Birkbeck/And Other Stories sample translation competition. Her translations have appeared in *Asymptote, El Núvol, Suelta, Palabras Errantes, The Washington Review, Two Lines Press, MPT,* and *Revista Machado*. She is now working on her first book-length translation for And Other Stories.

Jethro Soutar is a translator of Spanish and Portuguese. He has translated crime fiction from Argentina and Brazil for Bitter Lemon Press, and his translation of *By Night The Mountain Burns,* by Juan Tomás Ávila Laurel, will be published by And Other Stories in late 2014. He recently co-edited *The Football Crónicas* for Ragpicker Press.

Jon S. Vincent, a Colorado native and fly fisherman by heritage, completed his BA and PhD at the University of New Mexico. He was a Fulbright Fellow in Portugal and a Fulbright-Hays awardee for research in Brazil before joining the University of Kansas faculty in 1967. He served as Director of the Center of Latin American Studies, Chair of the Department of Spanish and Portuguese, director of various study abroad programmes, and was known for his dynamically entertaining teaching style until his untimely death in 1999. Among his major publications was a much-acclaimed monograph on João Guimarães Rosa (1978). His passion for Brazilian studies is reflected in *Culture and Customs of Brazil* (2003), published after his death with the help of fellow Brazilianists. His presentations in the U.S. and abroad promoted cross-cultural understanding and an appreciation of diversity.

Special Thanks

The editors would like to thank Agnieszka Piotrowska, the Polish translator and Arabic literature scholar who introduced Toni Marques to Hassan Blasim's literary world, and also Hassan Blasim himself. It was thanks to them that Toni and Comma came together to work on this project.

The Book of Tokyo
978-1905583577
Edited by Michael Emmerich, Masashi Matsuie & Jim Hinks
Featuring:
Hiromi Kawakami, Shuichi Yoshida, Toshiyuki Horie, Kaori Ekuni, Osamu Hashimoto, Banana Yoshimoto, Mitsuyo Kakuta, Nao-Cola Yamazaki & Hitomi Kanehara.

The Book of Gaza
978-1905583645
Edited by Atef Abu Saif
Featuring:
Atef Abu Saif, Abdallah Tayeh, Talal Abu Shawish, Mona Abu Sharekh, Najlaa Ataallah, Ghareeb Asqalani, Nayrouz Qarmout, Yusra al Khatib, Asmaa al Ghul & Zaki al 'Ela.

The Book of Istanbul
978-1905583317
Edited by Gul Turner & Jim Hinks
Featuring:
Nedim Gursel, Mehmet Zaman Saçlioglu, Muge Iplikci, Murrat Gülsoy, Sema Kaygusuz, Turker Armaner, Özen Yula, Mario Levy, Gönül Kivilcim & Karin Karakasli.

The Book of Liverpool
978-1905583096
Edited by Maria Crossan & Eleanor Rees
Featuring:
Ramsey Campbell, Lucy Ashley, Dinesh Allirajah, Frank Cottrell Boyce, Margaret Murphy, Eleanor Rees, Tracy Aston, Beryl Bainbridge, Paul Farley, James Friel, Clive Barker & Brian Patten.

The Book of Leeds
978-1905583010
Edited by Maria Crossan & Tom Palmer
Featuring:
Martyn Bedford, Jeremy Dyson, Ian Duhig, Andrea Semple, M.Y. Alam, Tom Palmer, Susan Everett, David Peace, ' Shamshad Khan & Tony Harrison.